THE TIGRESS

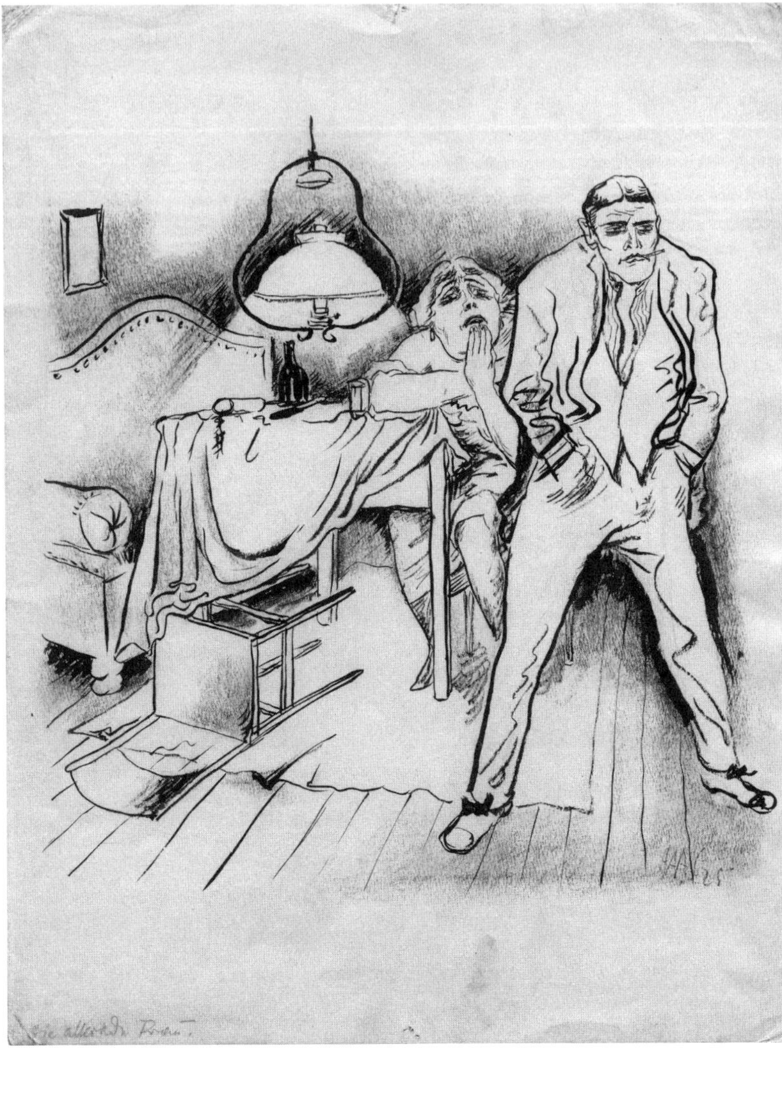

Walter Serner

THE TIGRESS

A Curious Love Story

with additional texts from Alfred Döblin, Theodor Lessing & Walter Serner

TRANSLATED BY MARK KANAK

TWISTED SPOON PRESS
PRAGUE
2025

ISBN: 978-80-88628-09-5
ISBN: 978-80-88628-37-8 (E-BOOK)

The work of the translator was supported by a grant from the German Translators' Fund as part of the program NEUSTART KULTUR by the Federal Government Commissioner for Culture and Media.

NEU START KULTUR

Die Beauftragte der Bundesregierung für Kultur und Medien

CONTENTS

I

No one knew what he actually did for a living, which was a prerequisite for being taken seriously in the influential circles of Paris. The fact that Fec was never seen gambling nor ever clearly in the company of a woman, in short never in one of those situations that would at least give some indication of a possible income, had the generally unfortunate consequence that he was not taken seriously. He was regarded as one of those base idealists who peddle between Fourier and Bakunin, earning a meager income from some dark intrigue, or as a deplorable dilettante clandestinely devising some subversive scheme, or maybe as a small-time hustler whose special forte would be exposed one day, or a lowly worker even — but many took him for nothing more than an arrant fool.

So when Fec was suddenly seen at the side of the beautiful Bichette, who was openly showering him with all the signs of her wild affection, it was met with great and widespread astonishment. And after a few days there was no longer any doubt the unbelievable had happened: Bichette had found her master, Bichette, the Tigress, had been — tamed.

She had received this sobriquet not only because it was generally apt, but because she fully personified it: she was depraved, cruel, insidious, often vile, and possessed of an unbridled desire to play the vagabond. She had copper-red hair, black eyes surrounded by a bluish white, and endowed by nature, at least in part, with those discordant colors the Parisienne applies as makeup. Skirt and blouse were her attire at all times of the year, rarely a scarf, and never a hat. While her voice, even though gravelly, was incisive and of a rare sensuality. She spoke only in argot, which she embellished with a host of idiosyncratic expressions. Three men had gone to prison on her account, two had shot themselves, and the rest of her countless lovers, all of whom she had cast aside after a few nights without being the least impressed by their threats or pleas, would have returned to her at the slightest sign, willing to put up with anything, without exception. She was despised by her colleagues because she never asked for money. The men foisted it on her, or expensive gifts, or, more or less, whatever they had. Her pride was boundless, her mockery monstrous, and a scarcely perceptible smile was enough to provoke her to tear into you, no matter who you were, and with a prowess that was truly awesome. So for Bichette to fall for a man, even if only for a short time, something that happens to almost every woman at least once in life, was virtually unimaginable.

Needless to say, this relationship produced a frisson of excitement in the cafés of Montmartre. Everyone wanted to know what was behind it. Audacious theories buzzed around the tables. All were rejected as being too primitive or too vulgar, especially with respect to Fec, who had suddenly risen in esteem in the eyes of all, and was now regarded as a person of the highest caliber, from whom one might expect not just everything, but perhaps even undreamed-of things.

Undoubtedly there was a chance Fec might live up to these expectations, while absolutely no reason existed to believe he would: Bichette's capitulation had occurred under conditions as simple as they were banal.

•

It had been at the Léon, a small brasserie on Boulevard de Clichy frequented only by hookers, pimps, and other youth of similar bent.

At around four o'clock in the morning Bichette, in the company of a Japanese man more stockily built than is usual for his ilk, had downed four glasses of white wine in succession at the bar and then unceremoniously plopped down on a bench, bored to tears.

The Japanese man sat meekly beside her and proceeded to caress her strong petite hand, as if he were petting a dog.

She snatched it from him and clouted his head, nearly knocking him to the floor.

He remained silent and sullen, sitting motionless next to her, and stared vacantly into space.

Fec, who had been observing all this, motioned to the Japanese man to come to him, more out of boredom than ridicule.

He rose at once, more than happy to escape his unflattering situation.

As the huge body lumbered toward his table, Fec realized Bichette would take umbrage, and knowing how pugnacious she was, he was curious to see her reaction. While he occupied the Japanese man with small talk, he kept an eye on Bichette.

She slowly rose after a few minutes and strolled over to Fec's table, sashaying her hips along the way.

The Japanese man simply kept silent and shyly examined his grimy hands.

Fec nervously began to sing softly: "J'ai une femme qui aime les animaux, ça c'est rigolo, ça c'est rigolo . . ."

Bichette quickly and firmly grabbed him by the hair, yanked back his head, stared angrily into his eyes, and hissed, "Don't seem to know me . . . Who're you now, eh?"

Fec's scalp was aching in pain and he didn't answer, so she shouted at the Japanese: "How do you know this shnuk?" (A Bichette expression.)

The Japanese man remained silent, sheepishly biting his thin lips with his yellowed teeth.

Growing confused in the face of Fec's immobility, Bichette let go of his head. "Rotter! . . . And you, you yellow boob, just stay where you are." Rolling her shoulders, she then sauntered away.

The Japanese man wanted to follow her.

But Fec held him back, letting him know, for no particular reason other than giving in to an understandable fit of pique, that anyone who was often seen in Bichette's company would soon have business with the police . . .

•

The next night Fec was sitting at the same table.

Around four o'clock in the morning, Bichette arrived. Alone.

After a quarter of an hour she waved at Fec, who, seriously doubting her intentions, allowed a few seconds to pass.

Then he looked Bichette's way again, and saw her face and

mouth change to that particular expression all women display when they want a man. This was the decider. He got up, shoved his hands in his pockets, tiptoed through the tables, and sat down at Bichette's table, deliberately and awkwardly, without so much as a glance at her.

Bichette was smoking, her cheeks puffing out, she glanced at Fec's fingernails and said acerbically: "I'm no one's moll. Remember that!"

Fec remained still and growled, "I wasn't thinking anything of the sort."

Bichette curled her lips into a sneer. Then she exhaled a laugh. "Seems you haven't done much thuggery. You've got the hands of a deadbeat."

Fec smiled weakly. "If you want to come with me, alright by me. If not, I'll go."

Bichette briefly eyeballed him and was somewhat taken aback that he seemed to mean exactly what he said. Still she demurred. Her pride began to entertain the prospect that he might intend to humiliate her. But after giving it a bit more thought she considered another angle: her pride was telling her to subdue his machismo into submission just as she had with those who had come before him.

"Eh OK," said Fec, tugging at his cap.

"Stay!"

•

On the way out, Fec grabbed Bichette's handbag.

"Silver?"

"Yeah."

"Beautiful piece." Fec weighed it in his cupped hands. "Are you afraid?"

"Fraid?" Bichette blinked. "Nah, not me. You know . . . No one's gonna jack me."

Fec managed not to smile as the moment called for him to remain aloof. "Ah, some people always give the wrong impression. Most of the time they're taken for naïve."

Bichette kept silent for a long time. Finally she drawled, "Well, sometimes they just are."

Fec coughed and, realizing he was annoying her with all this, shot back curtly, "You probably love those so-called refined gentlemen."

Bichette twisted her lips in an ugly way. "No."

"Hmm. A so-called fine gent is also quite the bore."

"Like everyone."

"Even a refined gentleman?"

"Those guys? Total ass pains."

"Splendid!" With a grin Fec tugged his scarf tighter. "So you love — animals."

Bichette shrugged her shoulders contemptuously.

"Shnuk!"

"Eh, I didn't mean anything by it," said Fec quietly.

Bichette spat.

•

Bichette lived in a small, smoky room on the fourth floor of the dirty Hotel Aëro on Rue Puget.

She undressed at once, and at such speed any other man would have been flattered.

Fec still had his pants on when Bichette already lay sprawled naked on the bed.

Instinctively, he looked at her body.

Glancing to the side, Bichette asked softly, "Aren't I beautiful?"

"Yes." Fec undressed without hurrying.

As he sat down on the bed, Bichette grabbed his prick and parted her lips, wide and round.

He took her slowly and firmly in his arms . . .

At eight o'clock in the morning they were still asleep and had yet to say another word.

At nine o'clock Bichette said in a tremulous voice: "Leave me now."

Fec started to get out of bed.

"Sleep here if you want."

Without saying another word, Fec lay on his side and fell asleep.

•

They spent the following days together, without interruption. The nights, too. They barely said another word. Only from time to time Bichette stroked Fec's hand. Or she played with his hair. Or with his cap.

Yet on the fifth day, at around nine a.m., she burst into a fit of crying.

II

The matter was not quite that simple and ordinary. Henri Rilcer, known as Fec, had put it all behind him. He was done with everything. Even with himself. He lived, as it were, from day to day. Into the void.

At seventeen, he'd been the lover of a fat Jewish woman who had four brown folds on her neck, six on her belly, and three small children forever grubby. The affair lasted eight weeks. Her propensity for constant lying, as he ostentatiously pointed out, was what made her so endearing to him. Above all, it gave him untold pleasure to be so despised by his own family. Once they became resigned to it, he abruptly broke off the relationship. At the age of eighteen, he slapped his father for having the audacity to take a lit cigarette out of his mouth in the dining room, where smoking was not allowed. He was thrown out of the house. For two weeks he clerked for a lawyer, and then embezzled a small sum and disappeared. Later he would resurface here and there. In winter he could often be seen in fashionable health spas in Vienna, London, Berlin, Rome. He always looked elegant, was almost always alone, but never failed to leave a scandal in his wake. He was tall, slim, and cut a dashing figure, which just as easily could have belonged to a diplomat or an apache. He returned to Paris at the age of thirty, unrecognized by any of his former friends. He was done with everything now. He had put it all behind him. He now wore a casual gray suit and a dark green scarf around his neck. He slept with cheap whores or in stairwells and lived mainly from petty theft.

He'd been leading this life for two years. He lived, as it were, day to day. Completely into the void. And now he had slept with Bichette, just as he had with dozens of women before her. Compared to those experiences, Bichette was no more than the faint glimmer of a nightlight, so he found neither her beauty nor her wildness especially stunning. It presented him with an opportunity just like any other. It only had to present itself. He no longer went looking for life. He let everything come to him without having any desire to sink his hooks into anything. He'd had enough. When he stepped into the street around noon, or when he was drunk, he often wondered how he was even still alive.

Bichette's sobbing had taken him by surprise. Not because it was something new to him, but because as a keen observer and mistrustful to the marrow he had come to the unassailable conclusion that he was encountering something involuntary, that her terrible convulsion had been a compulsion. And if it was a compulsion, then it was indeed a breakdown. His wealth of experience told him that he only needed to make a single gesture and he would have Bichette in hand for good. Yet he had no thought of taking Bichette. That he did so anyway could be attributed to a very peculiar reason.

•

After her convulsive sobbing had subsided, Bichette ran out of the room scantily clad and did not come back.

Fec finally left the hotel and went to the Léon for breakfast.

Gaby, a model and coke addict who never seemed to sleep, sat down at his table and tried to pump him for information about Bichette. "Up so early? Already — been given the boot, eh?"

Fec held his tongue.

"Don't worry. She's bluffing. It's her reputation, you know. And all the little roughhousing that goes along with it." Gaby looked at Fec with round, shimmering whitish eyes that clearly seemed to be conveying contempt for his entire being. "But you . . . Why aren't you doing anything? Get something brewing! Nothing without a bit of bluff. You need some rackets going on. Some real hustles. Else you'll end up in the gutter like a miserable mongrel."

Fec blew cigar smoke into her face. "I'm not all that interested. I'm not all that interested in myself, either."

Gaby hammered the table, bursting into laughter. "That's just it, you jackass! You're doing nothing for yourself. People never take you for what you are, but only what you make them think you are. And you also have to pretend to be what you really are. How else are they supposed to know what to take you for, eh?"

Fec narrowed his eyelids a little with feigned nonchalance. "I'm well acquainted with what you're saying. That's because about a fortnight ago at Hotel Grelot I heard almost these very same words, the last time we . . . But I'm just not in the mood for it anymore."

"What an ass you are!" Annoyed, Gaby dangled her breasts over the tabletop.

"Eh OK, why should I have to keep proving to people what I am?"

Gaby smiled wryly. "Too bad for you." She suddenly took his hand. "How about snorting some blow with me?"

At this moment Bichette entered.

As soon as she spotted Fec, she quickly ran to him. Only when she was standing at the table did she notice that Gaby, who had forgotten about it in her surprise, was holding Fec's hand. She said nothing as she sat down beside him on the bench.

Gaby's eyes moistened with excitement. Then, very slowly, she withdrew her hand from Fec's, stood up, and walked off. After a few steps, she shouted, "Au revoyure, 'ssieurs dames."

Bichette's head flew back as she laughed derisively, suddenly fell silent, and then at once jerked herself up straight again. Her outstretched arms gripped the edge of the table motionlessly. Her nostrils flared. She blinked.

Gaby immediately came back, head tilted in disdain, and sat down squarely at the opposite table. "Eha, eha! . . . So so . . . Well then . . . Yes, love, loooovvvvve . . ."

Bichette suddenly grabbed Fec by the neck and pushed his mouth firmly onto hers.

Gaby howled, her hands clenched at her own neck: "Eha, eha! That's abracadabrantissimo! The Tigress — trapped! But who's going to feed her now, eh?"

A chair crashed to the floor: Bichette had sprung to her feet. She threw herself at Gaby fists first and sank her teeth into her hands with such force that she fell from the table to the floor, screaming.

When Gaby, face contorted with pain, stood up in a rage, Bichette had a knife in her hand.

Jean, the waiter, grabbed Gaby's arms from behind and pressed his head between her shoulders.

Almost simultaneously, Fec snatched the knife from Bichette, picked up her handbag, and dragged her into the street.

•

Outside, both could sense that no words would pass between them for a long time . . .

On Rue Démours, Bichette stopped in front of a small clothing shop.

A yellow wool cap hanging in the window caught Fec's eye. He went into the shop, purchased the cap, and crookedly and charmingly set it on the tousled hair of Bichette, who, thoroughly bemused, was waiting in the street. To his own amazement he realized he'd acted impetuously, in a fiercely buoyant mood, having walked the long way from Montmartre to the Étoile at Bichette's side in a state of dull satisfaction. He rubbed his chin with the back of his hand. Everything suddenly seemed incomprehensible to him.

"Bing, it even fits." Bichette twisted and turned in front of the mirror next to the shop. When she finally moved away, she smiled at Fec. He seemed unable to decide how, though he pondered the smile for several minutes.

Just then, Bichette grabbed his sleeve and pulled him, so stupefied he could hardly resist, into a bijouterie.

She emptied her handbag onto the counter, stuffing the

assorted little boxes, pins, and brooches into her blouse, and asked quickly: "How much for this bag?"

The bijoutier examined it carefully with a large magnifying glass. Finally pursing his pale lips, he whispered: "Two hundred"

"Three!" Bichette demanded peremptorily.

The bijoutier objected, nattered away for awhile, and receiving no reply, grumbled doubtfully as he tossed the bag into his safe.

Bichette practically snatched the banknotes from him and immediately shoved them into Fec's waistcoat.

The bijoutier dared not crack a smile. He simply politely opened the shop door himself.

•

On the street, Bichette, hands in her hair, quickly adjusted her cap in a store mirror. "This is the first one I've liked."

Fec now began to realize what she was going on about and said, as if only to hear himself talk: "It's English wool."

"Eh? . . . Oh, I think it's simply riche." Bichette took him by the arm and pulled him behind her.

Fec wet his dry lips. He suddenly became irate because he couldn't see her face. He stopped. "Bichette!"

She immediately turned around and was surprised he had stopped. Still holding his hand, she stepped closer to him. So close he could see his face reflected in her pupils.

Fec's forehead wrinkled under his cap as he muttered through his teeth: "What's all this about! We've been doing nothing but nonsense since morning."

Bichette withdrew her hand and took a step back. Her eyes narrowed. "And what of it?"

"I don't love you."

Bichette's lips twisted into a sneer. "I don't love you either . . . But I just can't stay — on idle."

"On idle?" Fec tried to catch her eye.

"Yeah. I need to have something going on." Bichette quickly pulled him to her. "This is all just little stupidities, I know that. Don't you think I . . . Bah, the thing with Gaby, that was just pride, anger, vanity, what do I know . . . And this morning, that was . . . It's just because I can't keep idling. And you, I know damn well you're just idling too. The way you're living, it's total bullshit. Slack it is. Totally slack. I just can't keep living like that, so . . . This is . . . idiotic, that's what it is. I'm not saying we should go in for the whole phony tralala thing, like those syrupy chippies and their pimps. It's just run-of-the-mill louche, the silly little hoodlum games, the disgusting lovey-dovey sham and gazing into each other's eyes and the deceitful brutality, this whole trade with heart and ass and . . . Rotter! I'm fed up with all the yak! I want something else! You've seen both my scars. Sure, fun, when *I* get rolling . . . But in the end it's *also* nada. Like everything else. I just can't take it anymore. Basta!" She pushed Fec away and just stared at a streetlamp.

"How old are you?"

"Twenty-eight."

"Really?"

Bichette smiled in a peculiar way, wrapped her arms around him, and together they walked on.

III

On a sudden, exuberant whim, they dined in a tony restaurant on Avenue des Ternes. Bichette, wine glass to her lips, asked: "Why did you buy me this cap?"

Fec cursed inwardly at the fact that he was blushing. "I . . . It just sort of happened . . . Maybe also because I . . . No, I really don't know."

Bichette's eyes narrowed in delight. "I believe you. I believe you because you're blushing."

Fec's started to grind his teeth as he slowly raised his eyes. "Listen, Bichette, I took the money . . . I took money from you, before I even knew what you would do . . . what you said outside the bijouterie . . . what you said just now. As if I knew . . . you were already thinking that way. I actually really liked that. And yes, this idling is idiotic. If you don't want anything more, if you don't want to do anything more, it would be better for you to turn the corner, into the sweet air. But it's different with me. It's been like this for two years now. Before that, I was up to all sorts of things. Until I just got fed up with everything. Everything. Everything. Everything. Then idling was almost a pleasure for me. Over the past few weeks, though, I've even gotten tired of that. Of course, without admitting it to myself. As for your sobbing today, I know what that was, too. Eh OK, if you must know: buying you the wool cap was exactly the same for me as the sobbing fit for you. These sorts of surprises keep you on your toes, I mean, that things won't keep going the way they are. I now have a choice — into the sweet air . . . or — to want something again, to do something again."

A distraught look came over Bichette's face. "Yes, Fec, yes, Fec, let's do something! Something new! Something completely new! . . . Let's do — *us!*"

"Do — us?" Fec said, dumbfounded to his very lips.

Bichette fingered her skirt like mad, her eyes flickering.

•

They had already created somewhat of a stir. Parisians are accustomed to a great many things that would cause a riot elsewhere, but a shoddily dressed couple in an upscale, fashionable restaurant would raise an eyebrow or two, even in Paris. While their countenances, immediately domineering over this milieu, so to speak, along with Fec's confident demeanor, had quickly disarmed the maitre d'hôtel, their vivacious conversation, entirely at odds with the establishment's etiquette, and especially Bichette's rather animated facial expressions, only served to once again attract unwelcome attention.

The waiter discreetly approached, and with an unmistakable nod slid a small plate with the folded check onto the table.

When he had positioned himself three steps away, Fec called to him. "If the maître d'hôtel does not apologize at once, I will send my card to the director."

The small plate disappeared in an instant.

The maître d'hôtel quickly appeared and humbly apologized.

Fec did not deign to even look at him.

Everyone present dropped their visible hostility.

Bichette tensely pressed her lips together. Her eyes were half closed as she said softly: "Fec, we'll do *us.*"

Fec laughed unabashedly, loudly.

This seemingly boorish display of triumphalism displeased a gentleman whose specialty was presumably displays of salon courage. He strode up to Fec, his knees smugly swaying, and asked very loudly when the express train to the backwater of Angoulême was scheduled to depart.

Fec went pale. His fingers shook. He acutely felt how much fun it would be to slap this fop. His brain was raging.

He suddenly stood up, and his voice echoed through the room as he replied in impeccable French and with the most amiable intonation: "Leave through that door and then go across the street to the travel agency where you shall be sure to obtain the information, provided as courteously as a native of Angoulême."

All the tables were busy enjoying their meals.

A very old gentleman approached Fec, a glass of wine in his hand, and clinked glasses with him. And a lovely young lady called from the back of the room: "Bravo!"

Bichette held her breath.

Fec now asked for the check.

•

They took a taxi back to Montmartre, tongues entwined, right to the front of Hotel Aëro. They stayed in bed until seven in the evening.

At Liberty's Bar on Place Blanche, much noticed and therefore blithely silent, they took an aperitif, then dined at a little bouillon on Rue Lépic.

Around eleven o'clock they appeared on the dance floor of the Moulin de la Galette. And they didn't miss a single dance. They danced until four in the morning. With each other.

•

It was "all clear" in the Léon when they got there. Only two old women were sitting in a corner, at the back.

Jean staggered in, sleepy and grunting. When he saw Fec, he smiled knowingly.

"Watch out! Gaby's on the warpath."

"Do you know something?" Bichette asked sullenly.

"Why? I'd tell you if I did."

Bichette was tired. Fec was tipsy.

They leaned against each other on the bench and smiled wanly. Bichette's smile slowly faded, just lingering around her eyes; Fec's stretched jerkily across his face before becoming unsightly and stiff.

Then he cleared his throat several times, the fingers of his right hand confusedly stabbing the air. "Ha, only a woman who washes at an open window will never fall into it . . . provided it's not her ruse. But even if it's not her ruse, she can still fall into it, because it's not a bad ruse not having one at all. You understand me, Bichette . . . By the way, I've noticed that boredom sharpens the senses while beefsteak dulls them. Something's always behind it. To succeed you first have to tease people. Then when they become stupid later and stuffed full, you corner them. Then you've got them. By positioning yourself behind them. Because they've got nothing else behind them. Or should we be surprised that all ladies love fat, sweet food and . . . and . . . confectionery . . . ?"

Bichette pursed her lips viciously, sat up snarling, and snatched her hand from Fec's. "Shnuk!"

"Eh OK." Fec snatched her hand back and pulled her to him.

"Let go of me!" Bichette shoved her feet against him.

"Wait!"

Bichette tried to bite his hands and failing that, spat in his face.

"For shit's sake!"

"Let go of me!" Bichette made one last frantic effort to free herself.

But Fec wouldn't let go. "From a paper lampshade . . ."

"So, let go of me," whimpered Bichette, collapsing.

"At the age of sixteen, she made herself a hat from a paper lampshade that was burnt on three sides, and with this she snagged her first rich boyfriend. Yes, that's how life works . . . Listen, Bichette, that wasn't my sweet laundress from Rue Nollet. I loved her terribly. When I say — loved, that means . . . She had something in her eyes, like you. Dammit it all! Different. But things were good with her. I could talk. Talk. Talk. Talk. Almost like now. And if I went for a walk with her arm in arm in the Bois, I felt fine. Dammit! Of course, I was not fine. But with her, I at least somehow felt why I wasn't fine and would never be fine . . . Listen, Bichette, I love you, too, or don't. I never, never, *never* really loved anyone in my entire life. Why? This is very easy to understand: because I would've been a horrible rhinoceros . . . But you're right, Bichette, I simply can't go on like this any longer either. Something has to give. Something must be done . . . Eh OK, Bichette, I know what has to happen first, what has to be done first of all. Can you guess? Yes, we'll do us. Make ourselves do it. You were ingeni- . . . ingenious. Listen, Bichette, we must — *love* one another! This absolutely must — *be done*. This is so easy to do when one well and surely knows as we do that it's quite impossible to love one another . . . You understand me, Bichette . . . you . . ."

Bichette's wiped his lips dry with her hand. "Fec, I'm begging you, please, come! Let's go, now!"

Fec pushed her away gruffly. Suddenly he grabbed her elbows, pushed her back, and hissed in her face: "Bichette, listen, I love you . . . And you love me . . . Deal?" Saliva trickled from the corner of his mouth.

Bichette's head wearily dropped onto his shoulder.

Fec softly spoke to her mouth: "Tell me, right now, that you love me! That you'll always love me! That you will want to!"

Bichette's head sank even deeper. As it did, she said slowly and loudly: "Yes, Fec, yes, Fec, I . . ." All at once she roared: "Deal!"

Fec howled, let go of her, and drank.

•

Little Pimpi, whose real name nobody knew, had been leaning on the bar, watching for some time, and now he sat down next to Fec with the intention of calming him down. He was the only one who thought Fec was neither harmless nor a fool.

"Kiddos, dirtied your mitts by the looks, yo? Where'd it happen?" Pimpi chuckled affably.

Fec grimaced, "Drink! And do something befitting your name!"

"In England you was. I don't much doubt it, esteemed master."

"Well, I did." Fec gargled wine. "You're never supposed to know exactly what's what."

"Yo. I'm all for bad memory if the job calls for it."

"Pimpi, great Pimpi, where's your canned meat . . . where's your . . ."

Bichette bent across the table and put both her hands on Pimpi's arm. "Help me get him out of here."

Pimpi, ears twitching slightly, gazed with aloof interest. "Where he live?"

"Barely two cigs from here," said Fec so calmly that both sat in silent amazement.

And suddenly, the broad, Herculean body of the Japanese man was standing before them, right in front of the table. His fists were clenched at his hips, his small iridescent green eyes riveted on Fec.

Bichette searched for her knife. She grimaced furiously when she recalled that Fec had pocketed it.

Pimpi, who was a bit off balance, greeted the Japanese man, whom he thought was drunk.

His stiffened hand delivered a powerful blow to Pimpi's neck below the ear, knocking him to the ground, unconscious.

Bichette let out a small piercing shriek and stood still, her whole body trembling.

Fec's eyes goggled. His chin twitched strangely as he quickly pointed at the table with his left hand.

When the Japanese guy slightly tilted his head forward to look, Fec grabbed his full wineglass and splashed the contents into his eyes. Almost simultaneously, he knocked over the table, leaned back against the wall, and kicked the Japanese in the belly with his right foot with such force the man stumbled backward, groaning, and fell over a chair, out cold.

Having been thrown to the ground by the force of his blow, Fec jumped up, shouted to Jean, who was rushing over and smirking, to get Pimpi away from there before the Japanese man came to, and out the door he ran with Bichette.

•

The damp morning air almost sobered Fec up; Bichette, who had immediately torn herself away from him, was particularly morose. Staring at the ground, she followed three steps behind him.

Fec took a room in the Hotel Puget, diagonally opposite Hotel Aëro, since he feared the Japanese man would come looking for him before too long.

Bichette threw herself across the bed, bone-tired.

Fec leaned against the armoire and stroked his cheeks,

smacking his lips. "How nice it would be if the building collapsed right now," he thought fleetingly, smiling to himself.

From the street below came the rumble of heavy carts. The whole room started to shake.

Fec pressed his hands to his ears, breathing in agony.

"So, you dare to cover your ears when I'm talking to you?" Bichette suddenly shouted, sitting up in anger.

Fec let his hands drop, grinning dully. "No. I did that because . . ." He nodded quickly toward the window. "What were you telling me?"

Bichette looked past him at the wall with a proud absence of expression. Then she shrugged derisively and dropped her head on the pillow.

For just a few seconds, Fec sensed what it was she didn't want to repeat to him. But he was unable to commit this feeling to memory, even though he tried to again and again. He remained standing by the armoire, motionless, until his eyes started to burn.

IV

Around one o'clock in the afternoon, they were awakened by Pimpi.

Fec dressed quickly and opened the door to him, astonished. "How did you get here?"

"Loute knew the address." Pimpi placed a large leather bag and an equally shabby valise on the table, sat down happily, and, caressing the spot where he'd been hit, shook his head indignantly.

"This hotel?" Fec asked dumbfounded.

"The Aëro. Gaby coughed it up to the Jap."

Bichette rubbed her eyes with a corner of the duvet and propped herself up. When she saw Pimpi and her bags, an expression of alarm spread over her listless, fatigued face.

Pimpi's face mirrored the same expression.

Fec didn't move and intently observed: something extraordinary seemed to be afoot.

Then Pimpi let out his favorite Negro laugh, which he had nearly perfected. "Kiddos, this not so important, where everything . . . Nothing's happened, Bichette, nothing . . . I was just at the Aëro wasn't I. I thought you be clever and make a change, beautiful lass. And I do know don't I how much women need their seven things, so this I did . . . But very agreeable to me to be paid, because otherwise . . . etcetera, etcetera. Does the Parisian know? Yes, he does."

"Merci." Bichette's face, which had tensed up anxiously, relaxed again. "We can stay here for the time being, Fec."

"*We?*" Pimpi's fingers twitched and left his knees. "I beg *pardon,* I wasn't so sure."

Fec smiled understandingly. Then he took a closer look at Pimpi.

His head began to shake again. His prematurely aged face was visibly searching for a fitting expression.

"You know Pimpi, it does seem you're quite the moron," Fec snorted.

Pimpi muttered something, of which Fec could only make out "skinny herring." Then he said, jokingly: "Yo, the stoopid do make world pretty place."

Brushing past Pimpi while snapping his fingers by his ears, Fec went to the window and opened it.

Seeing the gesture, Bichette sneered.

Just then, Fec jumped back. "The Japanese guy is down there."

"Where?" Bichette jerkily slid to the front of the bed.

"Back!" Fec pressed himself behind the window curtain. "I can watch him unnoticed from here . . . Didn't you say, Pimpi, no one over there said a word . . . ?"

"Yo, I did." Pimpi rolled a cigarette nervously. "Maybe very good to avoid street awhile and go back into woods. And more . . ."

"He clearly doesn't know what he should do."

"And more . . . ," Pimpi failed to fake an innocent face. With his forefinger, almost shyly, he combed his pomaded hair onto his forehead. "You know, Bichette . . . that Goux, Laroche, Cauler the lot of 'em, nothing else happens if you alone. But now . . . it's different, very different, is what I say. And then Harry. Him you know. And then Ralix, the dog. Out in three days yo."

"He's going down the street." Fec, who had heard everything, sat on the table, eyeing Bichette, who was staring at the floor motionlessly.

"Or Bichette, go away . . . for a time alone." Pimpi was immediately annoyed at this suggestion. He threw his cigarette into the bucket so that it splashed, and he vigorously shook hands with Fec and Bichette. "I like very much this herring. He knock out big Jap and bleat not a word of it and also not how yellow ape do me." He took his hat from the tin candlestick. At the door he turned to face them. "If you need something, not coin, little Pimpi still sleeps at the Fécamp. So goodby." He slammed the door behind him.

His Negro laugh reverberated through the stairwell.

•

"I don't think it was Gaby who put the Japanese guy onto us," Fec said after a while.

"The way she got under my skin, not all that nettly."

"A sort of female Pimpi."

"Just not as sincere."

"Like I said — female . . ."

Bichette grabbed Fec by the shoulders, pushed him down on a chair, and smacked him in the eye: "*What* are you getting at, eh?"

Fec remained disdainfully silent, shoving his hands into his pants pockets.

"You think me and Pimpi . . ."

Fec looked aside indifferently.

"That's over. Ancient history. Or do you think I'm hiding all kinds of . . . ?"

Fec's lips moved mockingly. "Did I ask you for anything?"

"I want an answer! . . . No, but you acted as if I . . ."

"What's all this about!" Fec nodded reluctantly.

Bichette, whose eyes remained fixed on his face, gripped him tighter. "Or maybe you think I . . ."

"I don't think anything. That was never a weakness of mine."

Bichette gulped and let go of his shoulders. She undid her crumpled skirt, let it slip off, and stepped out of it. Then she put the washbasin on the chair and poured water in a wide arc. "Fec, I don't know if you remember what you said yesterday . . . this morning at the Léon . . . Please, hand me the towel! . . . Do you remember?"

"Yes."

"Every word?"

Fec, who was polishing his shoes, nodded.

Bichette finished her toilet in silence.

"Why are you asking?" Fec looked at her strong, long legs.

"Couci-couça." Bichette took off her dirty blouse, threw it to the floor, let her short silk dessous fall, and climbed onto the dresser to get a look at her nude self in the mirror.

Fec grew irate. "I was drunk."

"You seem to be apologizing." Bichette quickly turned to face him. When she saw him standing there, almost confused, she jumped down, laughing scornfully.

"He's apologizing! Rotter!"

Fec smiled reluctantly. "Mustn't I?"

Bichette played with a string in one hand, she caressed her breast with the other. "No."

Fec was astonished. "No? Really?"

"No." Bichette's eyes roved over him inquiringly.

"Really?"

"No." Her eyes stopped with a flat expression.

Fec was so curious that he laughed uncertainly. "Eh OK, so it's settled then?" Yet an embarrassing awkwardness suddenly came over him as soon as he had asked the question, compelling him to avoid Bichette's gaze.

Bichette polished her nails indifferently. "Yes. But . . ."

"But . . ."

"I . . . I don't know . . ."

"What?"

"Not quite . . ."

"What!"

"How you . . ."

"What, for God's sake!"

"What you think of all this . . . how . . ."

"You're not being sincere."

"Huh? Not sincere?"

"That's right."

"Rotter!" Bichette slammed her fist on the table so hard it cracked, and she began to wildly rummage around on it while continuously uttering half-words. At last she found the key, unlocked the leather bag, and threw a motley assortment of chains, bracelets, necklaces, and etuis onto the table. "There, there, there, there . . ." Her twitching fingers tore open the etuis and emptied them like bags. Earrings and diamond rings rolled around. Some fell to the ground. "You think . . . I like this sort of crap? No one's ever caught me wearing such junk."

Fec stepped toward her, and seized by a dull fury that confounded him, punched her in the shoulder and threw her onto the bed.

Bichette leapt up with animal-like agility.

And just like that, they were already tussling. Viciously. Tenaciously. Panting. But not hitting each other in the face.

A crystal-clear shrill cry that sounded ominous made Fec let her up.

Bichette stood up, breathing heavily. Her arms hung limp, as if all broken. Her black silk stockings were torn. Her red, scratched breasts heaved and trembled. Her complexion was earthy. The heel was missing on one of her shoes. She began to stagger.

Fec, almost frightened, embraced her with both arms and laid her carefully on the bed. "What's wrong . . . What is . . ."

Bichette weakly shook her head no. Then she slowly pressed her hands to Fec's cheeks, pulled him down onto her, and kissed him long and passionately on the mouth.

•

Afterward, they dressed in silence.

After some hesitation, Fec picked up the jewelry, put it carefully in the leather bag, locked it, and was about to put the key next to it on the table, when he felt the need to look to the side.

Bichette's eyes were trained on him, observing.

Fec shrugged his shoulders and pocketed the key.

Bichette laughed vaguely and hugged him. “So, now tell me how I wasn’t being sincere.”

“Not because you don’t know what I’m thinking, but . . . dammit all, what’s the point . . .” Fec pulled away reluctantly.

“But . . .” Bichette stamped her foot. “I want to know. So . . . but . . .”

“. . . but because you’re afraid you might not be able to go through with it.” Fec didn’t know why he was even saying this.

Bichette stepped away from him. “Maybe.” Her body’s motion pulled her hand from Fec’s shoulder. “Though I assure you it wasn’t quite like that. Anyway, it all needs to be discussed in more detail. Then I’ll know if I can. Just don’t think I’m weak or insincere. I still spat it all out to you.”

Fec suppressed the smile that had begun to form when he saw how Bichette’s eyes were racing.

“We have to decide quickly now, Fec.” Bichette began to hastily apply makeup. “Pimpi’s right. It’s best to disappear. At least for a while.”

“Hmm. How about — to Bagnolet.” Fec’s voice gave the impression he was in a bad mood.

“Out of the question.” Bichette’s fingers parted her magnificent hair and a jerk of her head threw it back. “Paris is still Paris.” She powdered her chest and neck with such vigor that a white cloud formed around her. “Nice.” What do you think?”

“Nice? Eh OK.” Agreeing made Fec nervous, even though he hadn’t considered Nice, nor was it, in his opinion, particularly inevitable. “A bracelet’s still lying there.”

"Sell it." Bichette's hands zipped about her head as she stood at the mirror. "And come back quickly." Gently dabbing, she powdered her nose, cheeks, and forehead. "Or we won't have enough." She corrected the lines of her lips with the tip of her tongue. "In the meantime, I'll eat here. Arthur will fetch something for me." She turned around with a smile. "Am I pretty like this?" Her smile triumphantly filled the room.

"Yes." Fec buttoned his jacket and wrapped the scarf around his neck.

Bichette's face darkened. "That's how you say it . . . like that . . ."

"You know you are." Fec pulled a yellow pack out of his pocket and drew a cigarette.

"Get going then!"

Fec smoked unhurriedly. "How long are you going to hang around here?"

Have you forgotten about the yellow ape?" Bichette sat down on the bed, tugging at her fingers. "Hurry up then! And be careful! Don't expose yourself unnecessarily!"

"I'm going to Rue du Temple. Old Chabert pays the best. But he haggles. This might take a while." Fec opened the door sullenly.

"Fec!" Bichette jumped up, threw her arms around his neck, stroked his head, and offered him her open, fragrant lips.

Fec kissed her slowly and for as long as she wanted. Then he left without a word. As he stepped onto the stairs, he didn't have a care in the world.

"Hold on!" Bichette called to him through the door. "I've still got two skirts over there. And three pairs of shoes."

•

Darkness had already fallen when Fec, slightly drunk, returned.

Bichette was lying on the floor on her stomach, drinking wine and smoking.

Fec stepped over her legs.

"Oh, it's you." Bichette turned her head upward, smiling.

Fec threw her skirts on the bed and her shoes on the floor. "Was anyone here?"

"Who should've been here?" Bichette stubbed out her cigarette on the floor.

"Just asking." Fec dropped wearily on the bed.

"How much did you get?"

"Five hundred."

"So, we're going." Bichette pushed herself up. "You smell like rain."

"Yes, it's raining."

Bichette stepped close to him and looked him in the face. "And like cheap brandy."

"Dammit it all!" Fec got up. "Let's go right now."

"Well, that's what I've been waiting for, you . . . rhinoceros." Bichette pinched him playfully on both cheeks and spat three times on his lips.

•

The night express was due to depart in forty minutes.

The valise was packed in no time . . .

As soon as the taxi drove off, Bichette, as if seized by a

wave of intoxication, jumped on Fec's knees, pressed her hands firmly to his head, and said in a lustful whisper: "Fec, now you belong to me. Me alone. And I belong to you. To you alone. Oh, we did a great thing! And we're going to do everything. Everything. I understood you perfectly. And you also understood me perfectly. We won't tralala. We'll stay sharp. We won't fool ourselves. We'll do it *all*. Make it firm and clear, yes, make it, make it . . . make it, bake it, cake it, cook it, cook, cook, cooking . . ." It was as if she were stuffing all the will she possessed into that butchered word.

Fec was completely carried away with unspeakable pleasure as he inhaled her breath. He shivered as he said her name: "Bichette . . . Yes, the things that weaken others and eventually turn them against one another and run them aground, those things will give us strength we can hardly imagine. The greatest strength. The ultimate élan. Firm to our marrow and clear as the nothingness on which we alone build, never being weak, never stupid. And if we should founder (since nature, life, is the dumbest, crudest thing that exists), it will not be because of us, we won't do it to ourselves. And this is what ruins not only the life but also the death of others: the dull awareness of not having done everything to avoid defeat, of having been weak, stupid. *Our* demise will be very different. Perhaps with that bright, sharp cry on your lips that you . . . Bichette, Bichette, please smack me!"

Bichette did so, without thinking twice. And she squealed with pleasure.

V

They had barely stepped onto the station platform when they were unsettled by the sight of Nice spread out before them in the white morning sun. Both felt the absence of the hostility that in Montmartre had enveloped them like a burning coil with its hundredfold hatreds and parlous lifestyle. Here it was calm and serene. Each felt they were already drifting apart, that this warm, bright city was coming between them.

They took a room in a hotel near the station, and even though they had slept most of the journey, they went to bed immediately merely to conceal their pique at each other.

Like all women of her kind, Bichette was passionately fond of bed, and she fell asleep after a few minutes. No matter what time of day or night, she would fall asleep as soon as she hit the bed.

Fec slept poorly and awoke after two hours. For the first time since he had been with Bichette, he felt alone again. He observed the woman lying next to him with an indifference that almost irritated him. Even so, his first thought was: not to wake Bichette, so that he might be able to enjoy his solitude. He shifted his body comfortably, with his hands behind his neck and listened, eyes open, to the noises slowly rising from the street below. He listened and listened. Where was that other sound? The familiar? The dull, tumultuous roar of Paris? He wondered why he found it so hard to do without that city, why the sight of Nice, where he'd so often spent enjoyable weeks, virtually disgusted him. Where was that ultimate spirit of adventure that had made him feel utterly pathetic on the ride to Gare de Lyon? "What a pleasure habit is!" he had literally said to himself. But he opened his eyes wide and fixed them on the ceiling: what was this tired, silly impulse he was allowing to govern him? Two empty tepid years in Paris and his tenacity, which had once accepted every change of location, every change of climate without missing a beat, was now depleted. But he knew that all it took to be rid of this condition was to want it, he only had to want it . . .

He suddenly clenched his teeth. He had recognized, down to the smallest detail, the danger this change of location posed to his union with Bichette. When he woke up, he observed her countenance, that proud, scornful look only she seemed to possess. He saw himself with her in the streets, the restaurants, the cafés, and he saw the onset of a terrible boredom. A substitute had to be created here, without delay, for the hostile life that had surrounded them in Paris. Every idyllic moment, every hint of sedentary life, had to be stopped in its tracks. Something had to be done at once. He had to take the initiative. He had to do something.

He gingerly climbed out of bed.

Well what? What should happen? What should he do? What shouldn't end?

Fec convulsively gripped a chair with both hands. He wasn't able to think of a single thing. Desperately, he bit one of his fingers and pressed his eyelids together.

"I . . . I do *want* something else," he finally said to himself contemptuously, and felt how it calmed him down. "Yes, but *why* do I want it? Because I don't want to lose Bichette?" He imagined the sleeping woman as dead, and found the idea agreeable. "Or because I want to use the capital this woman represents to provide me with a quiet life for myself later?" He breathed in the warm room, and in the soft armchair he felt himself growing angry with the tedium of it all. "Or is it because I want millions and the power it brings? Didn't I almost have it before?" He saw himself in Rome and a woman on a carpet . . . and in the attic of the house on Rue de Chéroy, where he'd spent the night before the first encounter with Bichette, waking up without a sou and grinning at his lack of desire. "So, why the hell? Why? Why? Why? . . . Is it just to honor this splendid deal? Splendid! Truly splendid!"

He was still gripping the chair.

Bichette rolled over on her other side, purring.

Fec anxiously let go of the chair. And suddenly saw clearly. So clearly that he closed his eyes for a few seconds to savor it. "It's my last adventure. My very last. And it will end like all adventures. Banal and grotesque."

"Like all adventures," he repeated in a low voice as he descended the stairs.

•

Fec didn't return to the hotel until seven that evening.

Bichette was still asleep.

After he'd meticulously made all the preparations, Fec turned on the light. He had to wake Bichette. Paying her no mind, he began to change clothes.

"Well . . . Oh . . . So, what's that . . ." he heard Bichette's voice faintly behind him.

"Put on the dress that's on the bed! There's the cloak, here's the shoes and the hat. Hurry up, we have to be at the casino in an hour."

"Yeah, what's going on . . . And you. What are you wearing?" Bichette's face expressed indescribably comical horror.

Fec knitted his brows to keep from laughing at the sight. "A tuxedo, I presume. Please, no questions right now! We've no time to lose. It's silly to talk while getting dressed. You lose time, charm, and your mind. So be patient! You'll find out everything you need to know on the way."

"So la-la." Bichette took a long, deep breath, languidly moving her head back and forth.

Suddenly pleased with himself while tying his tie, Fec heard Bichette take a few quick steps.

"And what's with the crap over there, eh?" Bichette pointed her chin contemptuously at the jewelry spread across the table.

Quick as a blink, Fec turned around and looked her in the eye, smiling to himself, but nonetheless resolute: "That crap is for you to wear."

"And if I won't, what then, eh?"

"You will!" Fec's fingers slowly balled into a fist.

"And if I won't?"

"You will!" Fec's fist rose a little.

"Rotter!" Bichette spat out.

Now Fec couldn't help but smile. "Bichette, I'm asking you for the last time . . ."

Bichette whistled cheekily to herself.

"Or . . ." Fec yelled, now infuriated.

"Or? Or?" Bichette was shouting, too.

Thrilled that it could all be over if he took this any further, Fec allowed himself to be assuaged by a pernicious curiosity. He quickly turned his back and began to tie his tie with great fastidiousness.

After a long pause, Bichette said softly, "Great. Just riche. Could be off about this, but sure seems like something's cooking."

"You're not off."

Not saying a word, Bichette stormed into the bathroom with diligent intent. Ten minutes later, she was sewing alterations.

•

In the taxi, Bichette curled her upper lip and pouted. "Too bad I couldn't wear those adorable shoes. But they were the right size."

Fec smacked his lips anxiously. "Does the dress fit?"

"You saw, except for a few little adjustments." Bichette slapped his hand, laughing gaily. "So tell me how you get the sizes right, how you always . . ."

"Now I'll tell you . . ." Fec spoke as fast as he could to keep what he had to say from becoming farce, which he was already sensing himself. "Now I'll tell you that you're a great beauty. A young duchess usually looks considerably more miserable. You are my mistress who is costing me a great deal of money. And you cannot say a word all evening. You are only allowed to move your head and your hands. That should be easy for you. It's safest if you act a bit flighty. Just always be mindful that you're a perfect lady."

"Merci." Bichette poked his chin with her forefinger. "You're cooking up something louche. No shooting, right?"

"You never know how things'll end up." Fec, now slightly offended by her ebullience, wanted to impress on her the danger of the situation.

"Bah." Bichette pinched his lips with two fingers and giggled. "The end is always some kind of — sweet air, esteemed master."

Taken aback and somewhat annoyed, Fec snorted.

In a completely different tone of voice, Bichette all of a sudden said: "Don't you feel like letting me in on what this is all about?"

"No."

Bichette only kept quiet because they had just turned into noisy Rue de la Gare.

•

It was past midnight when they drove back.

In the car, Bichette threw herself at Fec so violently she almost slipped off the seat. "Oh, Fec, that was quite riche! Richissimo, as Gaby would say. Who's that roly-poly anyway?"

"An old acquaintance of mine. His actual name is Jacques Laugier, and he in fact owns a dozen houses. It's a coincidence he was there. Or maybe not." Fec watched Bichette furtively.

"Yeah, but was it all *for his sake?*"

"No."

"I don't get it. The room was packed full. All that Paname elegance. Why all the fuss?"

"Very simple. Because I *made* it happen."

"You?" Bichette's face darkened as if she had been insulted.

"Of course." Fec looked at the driver's back with a grin. "After the shopping was done, I called the management of the Casino de la Jetée-Promenade as the porter of Hotel Ruhl to request a reservation for a front table for Baron Punschoff. Then I rang the editors of *Eclaireur* to inform them that Mistinguett was in Nice and intended to visit Casino de la Jétee that evening. And finally, I had a messenger boy deliver to the conductor of the Salle Privée orchestra a small envelope containing a five-hundred franc note and a few handwritten lines."

Bichette's eyes widened and became moist. "So *that's why* all the crazy commotion?"

"Even crazier when those five-hundred francs net a whole lot more."

Bichette threw herself on him again. Then she asked a thousand questions, kissed him wantonly, laughed, pinched, and bit, and didn't seem to notice that Fec was staring at her with a surprised smile.

•

In the room, Bichette didn't even take time to shed her cloak. "Fec, you really are brilliant! But word'll get out. Word'll get out, Fec."

"Not at all." Fec flirtatiously unbuttoned his glacé gloves. "I didn't foresee that you would be mistaken for Mistinguett.

Your name is . . . hmm, let's say — Thaller. Bichette Thaller. They basically fawn over anything foreign. It will make a very good impression that you were taken for this lady. But me, I *am* Baron Punschoff. This is the name I'm known by in some circles outside of Paris, and I only gave it up two years ago when I began to completely lose my appetite." Fec raised his eyebrows demonstrably and removed his gloves with a nonchalant toss.

Bichette, who had been listening impassively, sank into the armchair and scrutinized Fec with a leaden, glassy gaze.

Fec strutted across the room. He wasn't sure whether he should feel superior or not. But he was rather elated. "Tomorrow I'll buy the rest of the wardrobe we require, international hotel labels, and large suitcases. Well-pasted with travel stickers and cleverly scratched and scuffed, they'll look years old. Then they'll be brought to the storage hall at the train station with pickup two hours later from Hotel Ruhl, to whose very pleasant ambience I intend to move with you."

Bichette followed with eyes darting. "And that's what you call — retreating into the woods."

Fec took a giant leap in the air in front of Bichette, dropped to his knees at her feet, pressed her hands to her hips and woodenly and sententiously proclaimed: "'Tis a country road that promises the most certain success when one breaks from the woods."

"Bing." Bichette ripped his tie off. "Poor Paname!"

"No. The Promenade des Anglais will be our country road."

Bichette grabbed him by the ears, pulled him up to her exultantly, and gushed, "Bichon, you've struck gold with this rascal!"

"Not yet," Fec squeaked, removing her hands from his burning ears.

"Now tell me everything!" Bichette took his head in her hands and gently pressed her cheek to his forehead. "Everything."

"Everything?" Fec clicked his tongue and tried to get up.

But Bichette kept him pinned in a lubricious grip and wouldn't stop asking.

Fec enjoyed the interrogation and her hands, which suddenly offered up unspent tenderness. Aroused by them and virtually forced more sweetly still to her breathlessly waiting lips, he began to reply, and ultimately divulge . . .

They continued talking in bed. No less animatedly.

The occupant of the next room cursed and hurled a heavy object against the wall four times. To no avail.

When she finally got tired, Bichette laid her head on Fec's chest, who immediately fell silent. And shortly afterward, other noises could be heard.

Once again, in the next room, something loudly banged against the wall. To no avail.

VI

The following afternoon Bichette was already ensconced on a balcony at Hotel Ruhl, draped in a yellow silk peignoir, disdainfully watching the hustle and bustle on the quay and the small boats on the sea.

Fec, who had become listless and fatigued from the effort of moving to a new hotel suite, sat with his head in his hands, his eyes staring blankly into space, Bichette's back turned to him, such that he suddenly recoiled, oddly twitching, when she unexpectedly turned to face him. Only her eyes remained still and glittered icily.

After a time, which seemed interminable to both, they realized they were looking into each other's eyes.

Fec steadfastly met her gaze.

Bichette struggled to keep her composure for a few seconds. It was as if she were trying hard to suppress a certain expression. A strange color appeared on her temples. "What the hell's wrong?"

Fec forgot to answer, completely fascinated with the vehemence of her face.

Bichette gave him a painful jab in the ribs.

Fec flinched back in amazement. "What's wrong . . . ?"

Bichette's lips turned to a frown. "Something's up with you today."

Fec rubbed his sore side, smiling unwillingly. "Something's up with *you*."

"Me?" Bichette put her fingers under her chin. "Something's up with *you*."

"Eh OK, what?"

"Rotter!" Bichette, sensing she would inevitably say what she didn't want to say if sitting, shot up quickly and went into the other room.

Fec watched her, shaking his head. "Bichette, come here!"

She didn't come, but sat down to do her hair.

Fec quickly stepped behind her. "Don't you like this life? Are you bored?"

"No. I like it."

"Maybe my stories have robbed you of your élan."

Bichette put Fec's arm around her neck while she turned the curling iron over the flame with her other hand. "Must I really tell Monsieur Baron again how delighted I am at the return of his appetite? And all the things on which he has already partaken? If it were not for Laugier's indirect confirmations, I might not have believed much of what was confided in me last night."

Fec, trying in vain not to feel flattered, was stunned. "Maybe it would be okay to let you speak . . ."

"Bah, there's still a lot you don't know about me." Bichette, laughing more derisively than the moment warranted, pushed Fec's arm away. "Dips with such gifts to offer don't talk street. Besides, I spent two years at finishing school."

"Finishing school? You?" Fec belly laughed.

Bichette pulled the burning blades from her hair, humming.

"Seems I didn't make such a bad choice with you."

"Shnuk!"

"But you have to tell me all about it," Fec was still laughing.

"À la Saint-Glinglin." Bichette combed her hair vigorously. "Maybe you're just soused again, eh?"

"Sorry."

"What's my crap worth?"

Fec was silent for a long time, before slowly answering: "Apart from the pieces sold and those you need for toiletries, it should fetch around 45,000 francs."

Bichette threw the comb onto the marble surface. "More than any of your other women have had."

"But Bichette, you are . . ." Fec took her bare armpit in his mouth with both hands.

"Nettly, that is." Bichette jumped up. "Nettly!" She clutched Fec's neck, shook him so hard that his head wobbled, and blew laughingly into his eyes.

There was a knock.

The room waiter brought a calling card.

•

After Laugier had parted, though not before being invited to dinner, Fec and Bichette walked arm in arm along the quay.

They caused a sensation. An Austrian count pointed his walking stick at the couple and blushed at their indiscretion.

Fec smiled wryly. "Laugier is already mad about you. All the more because he thinks you're respectable."

Bichette managed to refrain from one of those insolent sways of the hip that had made more than one denizen of Montmartre blanch. "Respectable?" she finally chirped.

"I also told him today that I'm your first. If we pretended to be married, the allure would be much weaker. It's an immense advantage to be lovers. It also raises both our reputations sky-high and coats us in glue, so to speak."

"Huh?" Bichette, who seemed to be annoyed by something, pretended not to understand.

Fec had noticed the target of her question. "In glue," he repeated sharply, "so people stick to us, people . . . Laugier is already — stuck." Yet he was now struggling to find the necessary neutral tone, which meant that, inexplicably, he succeeded in doing just that. "He knows Flinsparker. Whom . . . whom you'll let take you — away from me. That's that."

Bichette felt her throat constrict. She stroked her firm breasts as if to smooth out the wrinkles of her blouse. "The one with the white hair and the moustache dyed black?" Her voice became very faint, and Fec certainly would have noticed it had a strong sea breeze not carried it away.

Fec's nose twitched. "My plan . . ."

"Tell me later!"

When he told her on a bench on the Place Masséna, Bichette listened in silence, then asked a few pertinent questions, and suddenly stood up.

"Are you putting down roots?"

Fec got up slowly, a little puzzled.

At that moment, Bichette kicked the side of a hound trotting past, causing it to yowl and lunge at her.

Bichette deftly dodged it.

Fec stepped quickly toward the dog, which moved away, wagging its tail timidly.

•

They appeared again for dinner in the Jetée's Salle Privée. When they entered, the orchestra broke off what it was playing and struck up *La Valse brune,* which had been performed for Bichette the previous evening.

No sooner was the champagne on the table than the spectacle repeated. The ladies paraded past below the balustrade with curious glances, which they often felt hardly necessary to conceal. The gentlemen kept a respectful distance, but always eyeing the fascinating couple. Only a few, overcome by her irresistibility, came closer to Bichette.

It had already been established that Bichette only danced with her beau or with professional dancers whom Fec paid well when he went out. He held this custom in high regard, which on the one hand nipped in the bud any suspicion that Bichette might be working for him, and on the other hand could be breached with all the greater success the moment a lucrative opening presented itself.

Such an interruption happened that evening. Fec invited Watt-Wayler, the young scion of a London banker whom Laugier had introduced, to sit at his table, and soon left, only to find it empty a few minutes later, to his deliberately poorly concealed shock and, ultimately, simulated stupefaction upon seeing Bichette dancing through the hall in the young man's arms.

When Bichette and her partner took their seats, everyone present paid close attention, but they failed to get their money's worth as Fec betrayed not a whit of jealousy, knowing full well that no one in the room would even dare to doubt the infernal suffering of his heart.

When Fec danced with Bichette again soon after, for the first time they were not left to dance alone, which until then, as if by secret agreement, had always been the case, but others danced even closer to them than was called for. The spell had been broken, and unleashed the curiosity that smelled a drama.

Laugier arrived late, apologizing profusely, and hardly dared to glance at Bichette.

For the first time she began to speak to him, which did it for him, and after half an hour she asked to be introduced to a young lady sitting at Flinsparker's table.

A short walkway into the main hall provided Laugier the pretext to greet Flinsparker and introduce Bichette, who was standing next to him. She immediately engaged the young lady in lively conversation and, leaving Laugier to Flinsparker, led her to Fec's table with little difficulty.

When Laugier followed, he was accompanied by Flinsparker, who jovially complied with Fec's request, expressed with deferential geniality, to join them at his table.

By the time they left, eight empty champagne bottles stood on the table, Flinsparker almost had tears of joy in his eyes, and Laugier and Watt-Wayler's minds were numb. Both noticed how Flinsparker had kissed Bichette on the bare upper arm as he held out her cloak.

Laugier only began to revive when Fec asked him to come back to the hotel for a chat.

Once there, he left him alone in the hall with Bichette, who, not without having complained a little about Fec beforehand, came on to him, as agreed, in such a way that he trembled in confessing his love for her. After feigning a protracted internal struggle, she consented to a rendezvous the following afternoon on the quay. She would come alone.

•

In the room afterward, Bichette, her lips pursed crookedly, pounced on Fec, tore off his collar and tie with such force they crackled, tore at his hair, screeching, shredded his shirt and vest, beat him, scratched him, spat on him, moaning and groaning.

Completely overwhelmed and beside himself with surprise, Fec allowed himself to be thrown to the floor.

As he lay motionless, he let her do anything and everything to him. "If she wants to claw my eyes out, I might let her," he thought, and confused by himself, stared into Bichette's raging eyes.

Spent at last, she slumped across him.

They lay like this for minutes.

Then she sought his lips and began to laugh maniacally.

•

That night turned out to be the wildest of all. There were moments when Fec no longer knew what to think. Bichette was on fire. And once she screamed with such ferocity the room waiter knocked anxiously at the door. But she said not a word. Fec also stayed silent.

Only near morning, as she was urinating, did she say, as if to herself: “Rotter!”

VII

As Fec was about to leave the hotel at midday to go shopping, a porter came running after him to hand him a letter that had just arrived.

Fec immediately returned to the suite: the letter had come from Paris addressed to Bichette Thaller.

Fec watched Bichette with lurking attentiveness as she read. She had barely finished when he asked gruffly: "Who from?"

Bichette skewed her mouth. "Pimpi."

"Pimpi? How?"

"I wired him yesterday."

Fec pounded his fist in his hand. "*Why* the hell did you have to tell him! Ah . . . !"

"Bah." Bichette's lips contorted in an almost impossible way. "Just wanted to know what was going on."

"That's, that's . . ." Fec kneaded his fingers, breathing rapidly. "There is nothing I stressed to you more than not to write any letters."

"I didn't write anything. And I can trust Pimpi."

"You! But not me!" Fec struggled to calm his face.

"Besides, I gave him the right address. I've nothing to hide."

"That means nothing. Show me!"

Without a word, Bichette handed him the letter. She shrugged her shoulders contemptuously several times while Fec read.

"Who is — Ralix?"

Bichette smiled wearily. Then she said slowly: "A slimeball."

"What?" Suddenly Fec's face calmed into pensiveness. "Ah, I remember Pimpi warning you about him. These threats prove he had reason."

"Blah blah," Bichette coughed casually. "A nutjob."

"Hmm. You have to admit, I know a thing or two about the habits of such types. If Ralix was heard bragging at the Léon that he could find you even if you were at the North Pole, he will under all circumstances try to make good on it."

"All the more reason to be kept in the loop by someone trustworthy like Pimpi."

"How do things stand with them?" Fec persisted after a pause.

"Pimpi and Ralix?" Bichette clapped her hands uncertainly. "Everyone knows each other there."

Fec pondered it. "Harry? It's not the first time I've heard this name."

"Bah. It's all the same shade of beige. Another one. I'd have my hands full there." Bichette threw herself on the carpet and dug her hands into the shimmering sealskin. "Though I didn't think Gaby would do something like that."

Fec's face shifted. "It was to be expected. They'll all jump out the window if they don't end up in an even more airy situation." He sat down glumly, angry with himself. "Tell me what you had with this Ralix!"

"Don't shout like that! . . . No. I'm not in the mood right now. And you're just way too puffed up for me."

Fec clenched his teeth and was about to leave the room.

Bichette looked annoyed and slid after him on the carpet. "Fec, what am I supposed do now?"

Fec looked at her, somewhat perplexed. "Go back to bed! I'm sure you'll be asleep in five minutes." He grabbed her under the arms, pulled her up, and carried her into the bedroom. With two fingers he slowly pulled her lower lip forward, giving her a quick peck. "Au revoir."

"Fec, Fec . . ." Bichette held him with both arms, breathing heavily, licking his lips, gums, tongue, rubbing her body against his in that very particular way until she felt it stiffen and throb. With a flick of her wrist she flipped her green silk kimono open and pressed Fec's face between her breasts . . . then further down . . . and further down . . . where it buried itself, moaning . . .

•

At four o'clock Bichette was strolling alone along the quay.

Laugier came running up, cheeks red, late again, and apologized profusely for quarter of an hour.

Then Flinsparker appeared out of nowhere.

After ten minutes of tortuous conversation, Bichette saw a verbena she just had to have.

Laugier stormed into the flower shop.

Bichette used this opportunity to express her annoyance at Laugier's *coincidental* presence.

So once Laugier had sweetly and smilingly presented her with the flower, Flinsparker led her to his magnificent Rolls-Royce Tourer that was waiting in a side street and featured on the hood, instead of the usual flag, a bronze figurine of a naked woman bashfully closing her arms over her bosom.

Bichette was enthralled.

Flinsparker beamed, and adroitly took his chauffeur aside.

Laugier shook in anger.

Flinsparker helped Bichette into the coupé, left the side door open, and hastily sat down next to the chauffeur.

Laugier barely had time to register what was happening when the car started to move and, with its door still open, glide away silently.

•

In the evening, during dinner in the Jetée, Fec proved to be perfectly clueless and joked so conscientiously that Bichette found it difficult to maintain the necessary aloofness toward him.

After dessert, Fec, who until then had danced only with Bichette, walked straight up to the table in front of the orchestra where Red Bia, the ballet star, was sitting with two professional dancers, and asked her for a dance.

This time he was left alone again to dance with her.

Thinking she had sussed the situation, Red Bia became animated and allowed Fec, whom she was merely obliging, to dance with her so intimately that in the eyes of the company sitting at Bichette's table it was nothing short of scandalous.

The whole hall was visibly indignant.

Although she had been informed of what Fec was going to do, Bichette was irked all the same, even if she was not quite sure why, and when he returned, she greeted him almost acrimoniously.

Fec didn't understand what was behind her improvisation, and he became tentative.

While it wouldn't have taken much for the little contretemps to escalate, what happened was enough to triple the effect Fec had intended.

This time Flinsparker settled the bill.

Once again he warmly apologized to Laugier, who was in the most cheerful mood thanks to the course the evening had taken: he had been convincingly persuaded that he would have gotten into the car as well if not for the misfortune of having noticed the open door much too late, and Madame Thaller would naturally be of the opinion that it was merely a misunderstanding.

Seated across from Laugier again in the hall, this was by no means her opinion, on the contrary, she was fairly embarrassed that Flinsparker had dared to use such an impertinent trick to be alone with her.

Laugier snorted.

Then he arranged a rendezvous for the next afternoon and was momentarily left alone with Fec, who appeared quite receptive.

Fec appealed to their old friendship and asked for advice: he did not want to offend Flinsparker, but could not tolerate the way he was seducing his mistress. It was almost unbelievable for a man of his position to take the liberties he had on the quay.

On his way out the door, Laugier solemnly promised Fec to give Flinsparker a stern warning.

•

At the door of their suite, Fec pressed Bichette about her behavior in the Jetée.

Bichette squirmed in torment. "I don't even know myself . . . Oh well, it didn't do any harm, did it."

"Bichette!" Fec put his hand on her bare shoulder and yanked her around. "What was that?"

Bichette glanced away. She seemed to be mulling things over. But then she slightly nodded her head, as if she didn't care what she said. "It was just suddenly so easy for me . . . I felt so slack with that bozo Laugier and that meathead Watt-Wayler and that dullard Flins of a Parker . . . while you . . . Yes, yes, I know. It's stupid. Bonkers. Whatever you want. But it was stronger than me. I just couldn't control myself. Now leave me alone."

While this whole conversation lingered in the air, Fec took malicious pleasure in making a confession of his own. "Listen, Bichette!" taking a step back from her quickly to avoid giving himself away, "when I read Pimpi's letter I . . . I felt the same thing."

Bichette let her cloak drop from her arms and looked inquiringly at Fec. "Bing. I already felt it yesterday on the balcony. It seems to be working out for us. Our love is showing."

Fec pretended not to have heard. He would bring it up later, sometime later when it would be more convenient . . . He jerked his head around. "Ha, it's amusing, isn't it, that everything has to be done by yourself? If you had appeared at the Jetée one evening, so delicate and guileless, without any publicity whatsoever, some gentleman, quiet in every way, probably would have fallen in love with you, or even the head waiter might've. But no one would be fighting over you.

Vanity needs to be provided with a stage and a gallery of spectators so that it blinds you. Blind to your own egotism. Egotism is not the final impulse. It's the effect. And that effect has to be created."

Bichette knelt in an armchair, eyes closed. There was a tinge of mockery in her words as she sleepily said, "You've talked like this twice before. Do you remember? The first time we went to the Aëro. And then when you were drunk."

Fec was quite aroused by her slumped form, and stepped behind her, grasped her breasts, and began to squeeze them, more and more firmly.

A gentle smile came across Bichette's lips, and she offered him her mouth. As his lips closed over hers, her eyes rolled upward, only the bluish whites visible.

VIII

When Bichette awoke she could sense Fec standing at the foot of the bed, and after blinking cagily to confirm he was there, she pretended to still be asleep.

Suspecting as much, Fec sat down slowly on the edge of the bed and gently stroked her hair and lisped, almost against his will: "My sweet, sweet Bichon . . . You solid, mighty animal . . . You dark, smoldering woman . . . You're the strong chain I hold onto to keep from falling, when I'm on the verge of falling . . . And I don't even know to what this chain is attached . . . If I did know, I would . . ." But he was then seized by a malicious desire. ". . . I would tell you, although I know you're not asleep and can hear me."

Bichette jolted up, her face contorted. "Shnuk!"

"Eh OK."

"Fec, that was . . . Oh . . ."

Laughing, Fec threw himself onto her, pressed her back into the bed with the whole weight of his body, and whispered before her furious eyes: "And you? Didn't you pretend to be asleep to . . . Shouldn't you have kept quiet and . . ."

"And . . . ?" breathed Bichette.

". . . and believed it?"

Eyes tightly closed, Bichette remained motionless for a few seconds. Then she wet her lips and breathed heavily and sporadically.

Only now did Fec release her, clicking his tongue three times.

•

They managed to avoid each other the whole day.

Laugier waited in vain for two hours on the quay.

That evening, not once did Bichette dance with Fec. This gave Red Bia the opportunity to perform duets to thunderous applause, which proved to be a great personal success for her judging by the considerable influence she visibly gained with the managing director.

A conspicuous incident occurred shortly after midnight. While Bichette was dancing with Watt-Wayler and Fec with Red Bia, Bichette's foot kicked the ankle of Red Bia causing her such pain that she yelped and would have fallen over if Fec had not been holding her tightly in his arms and carried her to a chair. The ankle quickly swelled. Bichette had accomplished more than she might have intended: Red Bia was incapacitated.

Fec calmly returned to his table, but at the sight of Bichette, who was looking at him contemptuously, he began to confront her, driven partly by such an intense animus it was unfamiliar to him, but partly as well for his own amusement, so reproaching her for being clumsy that it bordered on the implausible.

Feeling of a similar bent, Bichette replied with such insolence that Fec believed he had never seen her so brazen before, and when he answered her in like manner, she suddenly launched into her patois, releasing her otherwise subdued voice from its restraints to assail him with a stream of ferocious invective.

Fec saw at once that an unstoppable torrent had been unleashed, and suddenly enraptured by Bichette's wildness he let it transport him in profound delight. He thought of nothing, only felt what he would need to do, and stood there with his head slightly bowed, his fists clenched in his pockets.

Before him was Bichette, her hands on her hips, fingers spread, her bare elbows turned far forward, her mouth open, even if she wasn't screaming.

In no time a crowd of spectators formed around the table with Flinsparker, Laugier, and Watt-Wayler standing off to the side like referees.

No one who witnessed the fracas was able to say what exactly had sparked it. Suddenly Fec and Bichette were in each other's grip and scuffling like two street kids, each with the same engaging truculence and the same sympathetic hatred in their gleaming eyes.

Fec was on the point of overpowering Bichette when Watt-Wayler, who was the first to recover from the initial shock, remembered that he ought to be chivalrous. He grabbed Fec by the shoulders and tried with all his might to pull him off.

Fec, impervious to anything since he had touched Bichette, now flew into a rage. He released Bichette instantly and lunged at Watt-Wayler, whom he punched hard on the temple and flung with two quick flicks virtually through the air onto the table, the clattering glasses, bottles, and plates shattering on the floor.

Fec's face expressed such menace that no one dared to intervene. Yet mainly because everyone was mesmerized by the thrilling brawl and unconsciously wanted it to continue.

Watt-Wayler had meanwhile quickly picked himself up and planted himself in front of Fec in a boxing stance.

With astonishing dexterity, Fec leapt at him sideways, just missing his punch, then pounced on him and proceeded to pummel him mercilessly.

Enraged by his defeat in front of Bichette, Watt-Wayler managed to pull out his Browning pistol.

Only now did Flinsparker, Laugier, and the other onlookers realize it was well past time to intervene.

In a matter of seconds, Watt-Wayler was disarmed and Fec was dragged off of him.

In the ensuing tumult, Fec, suddenly without a foe, quickly sobered up, and with the help of a waiter was able to get Bichette, cowering on the floor, trembling and panting, out of there. He was astonished to see her knife being held in her drooping right hand.

While the waiter ran to hail a taxi, Fec took the knife from Bichette's hand, pocketed it, and carried her in his arms at a trot to Hotel Ruhl across the street.

•

Bichette, barely settled on the chaise longue, gritted her teeth, glared wildly at Fec, and turned her head toward the wall, spitting.

Fec pulled down her skirt, crumpled it up, threw it into a corner, and shouted: "Ah, is *that* what you mean by — not fooling yourself? Is *that* what you mean by — staying sharp? Haha . . ."

Bichette slowly sat up. She blinked.

Fec forced himself to calm down, squeezing his neck with both hands. "I've noticed for a while that you're beginning to appreciate the idiocy of inflated sentimentality. Your feigned sleep, for example, can be categorized as such."

Bichette stood up, wriggling defiantly. "Why did you have to beat up Watt-Wayler, eh?"

"Shut it! You're the one who started it." Fec felt how inappropriate and ridiculous his excitement was but was unable to control himself.

Bichette finally turned her face fully to him, exhibiting an astonishingly impudent childlike expression. "Well, I find these refined shenanigans that come to nothing boring and stupid. Basta."

"They've only come to nothing as of today. And thanks to you. You alone."

"Bah!" Bichette sat down again, dangling her feet.

Fec was suddenly boiling in senseless rage, and he shoved a chair toward her without hitting her.

Bichette stayed seated but stopped dangling her feet. "If this goes on for much longer, I'll go bonkers."

"Bonkers?" roared Fec. "Splendid! Better to be sensible!"

In the adjoining bedroom something fell, producing a short, silvery sound.

Fec blushed, having only now come to himself.

Bichette saw his blush and stretched out in thought.

Both were silent and seated in a position so that neither could see the other.

After about a quarter of an hour, Bichette crept up to Fec, slid onto his knees and pushed up his chin with her index finger, and laughed long and loud. "Fec, I think — maybe we do love each other. Don't you think so, eh?"

"Idiot."

"Merci."

•

Later in bed, Fec said: "I'd give a lot to know what's going on with us."

"Bing. Me too." Bichette pursed her lips with a smile.

"Can't you tell me why you kicked her like that?"

Bichette took her head in both hands and exhaled a tortured sigh. "Why? . . . Sssss, slack it is! . . . Well at first . . . at first I thought it was jealousy, that is, a jealousy in my head, that is, pure conceit, the whole thing just for the sake of those watching. You know how it is . . . But no, it wasn't that. Because just before I kicked her, it hadn't even crossed my mind to kick her. It was just like how a hunting dog acts. And afterward I was all gaga at myself that I did it . . . Oh, maybe I did it the moment I saw your head tilt toward me as you danced. I think . . . Yeah, I almost feel like that could be why I did it. But I just don't really know."

Occupied with himself, Fec hadn't been listening to her at all, which he realized as soon as she went quiet. So he said excitedly: "And it's a complete mystery to me that I . . . I, I, I, who so meticulously studied everything beforehand . . . our approach, every psychological detail . . ."

"Huh?"

"... discussed everything with you in detail, instead of just overlooking your faux pas, confronted you. As if I didn't, haha ... as if I didn't know in advance how it would end ... The rest is obvious, after all."

"Obvious? How so?" Bichette tugged painfully on his ear. "Couldn't you have just stopped yourself?"

"No." Fec sat up hastily. "No, I couldn't. The rest was just a matter of nerves. Perhaps if someone had laughed out loud just before I started whaling away at Watt-Wayler, or if someone had thrown a glass on the floor that I would ... But I don't think it would've been possible even then. You just can't fight nerves when they have the upper hand. That's already a problem."

Bichette shook her head, smiling strangely. "What is, a problem?"

Fec sank back on the pillows. "A problem is nonsense."

"So when Watt-Wayler flew onto the table and all that stuff fell to the floor, if only it could've been a few seconds earlier?" Bichette waited for an answer, diddling with her fingers. "Fec, listen! I think it was just like in Paris ... just like my sobbing fit and the yellow wool cap ... Bing."

"Yes," said Fec surprisingly quickly, thinking almost the same thing. "Just for a different reason. Before it was because we couldn't keep idling. Now it's *because* we're idling. Just *flat-out* idling. Essentially — the same thing."

"No, Monsieur Baron." Bichette hesitated whether she should say what she was thinking. But with a twitch of her shoulder she made up her mind. "This time it's because we're *no longer* idling, we're resisting it. Because our deal has turned into something else."

"Something else? What?" Fec asked with feigned disinterest, which he couldn't pull off because of the bad position he was lying in.

"Bing, a fact. We love each other. That's for sure. We just don't know — why, and not — how. That's also for sure." Bichette's whole body was triumphant.

Fec turned away. He smiled. Yet he was too tired to reply.

IX

When they woke up both were in a very good mood.

At breakfast Bichette asked, winking in fun: "And Flinsparker? Should I, you know?"

Fec acted as if hadn't picked up on the ancillary intent of her question. Quietly and thoughtfully, he replied: "You have to let yesterday's business — cool down a little, so to speak . . ."

Vexed, Bichette put down her cup. "By then it'll be too late."

"Why?" Fec did understand what she was saying. "Maybe it will work out, notwithstanding. Or even much better."

"Notwithstanding?" Bichette laughed breathily. "It'll never work out, notwithstanding. And even much better? That's just like you. It was supposed to be done *today*." Her eyes became wide and watery.

Fec smiled. "Today — you say."

"Yes. I said — *today*. I *said* — today." Bichette looked angrily out the window.

Amused, Fec looked at his plate. "Not only would it be all the better, it would be for the very best. There will be no more talk of a 'notwithstanding.' And certainly not of 'too late.' We couldn't have given the penultimate act of our jealousy farce a more spectacular finale than yesterday's melee. The fact that you turned out to be a true Montmartroise undoubtedly inspired Laugier and certainly aroused Flinsparker's curiosity. Watt-Wayler's wrath is irrelevant, and if he's not smart enough to keep it under wraps, Flinsparker will just have further incentive to make a decision and for Laugier not to accept that decision. I'm genuinely quite curious to see what those two . . . tomorrow, or the day after, these psychological allurements will . . ."

"Huh?"

"I mean . . . You're certainly beautiful, and you are . . . that's that. The surest way to persuade an American millionaire to do something foolish is to sell it in a way that not only makes it invaluable to him, but above all excessively flattering. All of Nice is talking about you and me today. And tomorrow, instead of me, they will be talking about — him. And when Laugier hears that, he'll do a lot, an awful lot, so that the talk is instead about — him. Eh OK. But later, when the scandal has cooled down (and it cools down very quickly after such a nonpareil climax), everyone also cools down. *Then,* at that point, it might be too late. It's even probable . . ."

". . . that it'll be too late then." Bichette flicked the plate away with both index fingers. "You're right. And you can be sure that Flinsparker when *I* . . . fun, when I get rolling."

"When are you meeting him?"

"At three." Bichette scooted her chair back.

•

To avoid the unpleasant encounters they were certain to have, they drove out of town.

Half an hour later, not far from Cannes, they stopped the

car, ordered the chauffeur to wait, and continued on foot along the seashore.

The trip had made Bichette noticeably ill-tempered, but so had the memory of the last conversations, especially of the previous night, which she knew would be continued.

Anyone who saw them would believe it was only by chance they each ended up in the same place together. It looked as if each were walking alone. Each waited for the other to begin.

Even so, they walked next to, in front of, and behind one another for about quarter of an hour until Fec finally broke the unbearable silence by uttering, unable to resist, the quite incomprehensible wish: “Give me a bean and I’ll tell you the sausage is blue.”

Bichette waited to see if something else would follow. Then she laughed, in a crass and loud way. “Don’t you think, eh, you should drop all this stuff you’ve picked up?”

Fec came to life with a glint in his eye. “That’s it! That’s it! Picked-up stuff! Picked-up stuff!”

Bichette laughed even more crassly and loudly. “Are we doing us, Monsieur Baron? Or are we not doing us?”

“That’s it! “We’re doing us.”

“Rotter! . . . What is it? Well say something already!” Bichette nudged Fec forward, grabbing his elbow.

Fec stopped immediately. “Weren’t you going on yesterday about the *fact* that we love each other? And that it was for sure we just didn’t know — why, and not — how? But if . . .” He paused, his hand on Bichette’s forearm, to heighten the emphasis of what he was about to say. “But if the why and the how are missing, what about the fact?”

Bichette pushed his hand away angrily. "Huh, what are you going on about?"

"This." Fec walked slowly, his hands clasped over his chest. "Neither you nor I were in the right. The fight in the Jetée didn't happen because we were *actually* on idle, but also not because we were *no longer* on idle. Our deal has not changed at all. It remains what it was."

"You know more than I do." Bichette trilled snippily. "What was it, actually?"

Fec paused. "Splendid!" Then he pulled Bichette's weakly reluctant arm under his own. "What did we agree on? It was, as you said in Paris on the way to the train station, that we wanted to make sure not to fool ourselves like others, not to do — the phony tralala — to stay sharp, firm and clear, with ourselves, so we can do it *all. That* was our deal. Nothing more."

"Nothing more?" Bichette drummed her fingers on his forearm. "And our love? Didn't you want to do that too, eh?"

"Back then, that morning at the Léon, I was drunk."

"And in the afternoon *you* asked *me* if we had a deal."

"Yes. But only after you challenged me."

"Couci-couça. You make it easy for yourself."

"*You* make it easy for *me*."

"What? How?"

"I accused you then of being insincere. Do you remember? And you really were insincere, too, Bichette."

"Me?" Bichette pulled her arm back.

"Yes, you. You suddenly became fickle, but you didn't want to admit it to yourself. That's why you created that scene with your jewelry, to force yourself, so to speak. After you'd already given me three hundred francs, there was really no need for you to prove to me that . . . Eh OK. That's the only reason I got so angry. Although it was only later I understood what this scene was all about. Even if I still don't fully understand it today."

"Bing."

"So, enlighten me!" Fec scratched his fingernails nervously. "Some things are always overlooked. Before and after and in the midst."

"You got that right." Bichette folded her hands.

Fec smiled arrogantly. "You were just afraid you might not be able to do it, and . . ."

"Me, afraid . . . ?"

". . . and said that everything still had to be discussed in detail. Of course, that was something I also needed. But we didn't discuss it because we left so quickly. By the way, I only went because I was sloshed at the time."

"You were sloshed when we left, not when we decided on Nice."

Fec felt embarrassed for a few seconds because he sensed he wouldn't be able to make this apparent contradiction clear to her. Then he continued angrily, "And we never resumed this discussion because the opportunity never arose, wasn't going to arise. Eh OK, it will never arise, either, the discussion cannot be resumed. Nothing else *can* be discussed. *That* is the crux. That's that. You seem to have felt this rather clearly, by the way, because on the way to the station in Paris it was *you* who formulated what I wanted, as it were.

"What *you* wanted?"

"Well . . . what I wanted, too. Because you were the driving force from the very beginning. At the restaurant on Avenue des Ternes, it was *you* who suggested that we do us . . . *You* wanted to go to Nice. And *you* wanted the deal, too."

"And you only went along with it all because you were drunk, huh?"

"Yes . . . and then also . . ."

"Fruitcake."

"Incidentally, your formulation contained an error."

"Which you will now dutifully correct." Bichette placed her hands firmly on her hips.

Her alluring figure was so distracting that Fec had to avert his eyes to avoid becoming muddled. "I literally remember what you said: 'You belong to me. Me alone. And I belong to you. To you alone.'"

"Did I say that?"

"Yes, you did."

"Then it was a mistake."

Fec was silent, somewhat perplexed. "Are you seriously suggesting," he asked at last, "that you belong to me?"

"No, no, no."

"Or that I belong to you?"

"Merci." Bichette sauntered across a field, insouciantly swaying her hips.

"Eh OK." Fec reluctantly followed, but dared not tell her which way to go out of fear of aggravating her too much. In fact, he spoke very softly to make sure she would continue to listen to him. "Basically, our deal is nothing but a kind of — mutual defense pact . . . A hideous phrase! But this is the only way to describe what . . . for shit's sake! This is why it can't have become something else, as you said yesterday. Still, something has changed. We've become, if not weak, then at least very stupid. Because this Jetée business was — incredibly stupid. Though hardly a surprise. All sorts of stupid things had already happened. Even the little episode when I first danced with Red Bia was stupid. Your behavior on the balcony when you said I'd changed was also stupid. But while I already knew back then what I'm telling you now, you indulged in sentimental notions of love."

"You're a total fruitcake!" Bichette stopped indignantly and stared insolently in his face. "Back then . . . ?" Oh, back then I thought something completely different."

Fec almost closed his eyes. "May I ask what?"

"You may, you mooncalf. What was I thinking back then, eh? Great! Not the same thing you were, that's for sure. But I thought the same thing . . . Bing, I thought I was already beginning to bore you, that you were already regretting it. When we went to the Jetée for the first time, I mean before at the hotel, you behaved differently. You were irritable. You were never like that before, please . . ."

Fec put a hand on her shoulder. "Bichette, stop it! When I mentioned 'sentimental notions of love,' it was . . . Well, this scene's not very clear to me either. Why are you lying though?"

"I'm lying?" Bichette pushed him away, stamping her foot.

Fec was undeterred. "You said on the balcony that you felt our love was showing itself. And you said it later that night, at the hotel."

Bichette shrugged her shoulders angrily and walked on, whistling.

Fec followed her slowly. When he caught up to her, he tried to make her walk close to him to calm her down. "So here's where things stand: we've acted stupidly. Mind you — *we!* Because I behaved like an idiot when Pimpi's letter came, and when I beat the daylights out of Watt-Wayler, I was . . . But while I could see more and more clearly where it would all lead, you thought you had to interpret my stupid actions, as well as your own, as if our deal had been shattered — given the fact that, haha . . . love had come over us. Stupidity! Nothing but stupidity!"

"Absolutely my opinion," said Bichette in a completely different voice. She made a noticeable effort to avoid Fec's closeness. "If you think about it, it's *all* stupid."

This preemptive assertion so annoyed Fec that he became increasingly vehement as he continued to speak. "Eh OK, the result! We agreed not to fool ourselves. So our deal was only something negative. You understand? Something to avoid. We should be firm and clear. Instead, we were reckless, we did the most atrociously stupid things. So it was our own doing that ultimately drove us into moods and excesses that suggestively drew us in, into it, both you and I fell under a . . . fell under a spell, as it were. *You* became completely addicted to it. I just remind you of how crazed you were after the first — haha — workday, when you tore off my collar and tie, and then rode yourself into a frenzy in bed, the pleasures of which were real, but the motives behind them, not at all. You did all that just to cleanse yourself of . . . so to speak, being sullied by work — haha — in an excess of love par excellence. Incidentally, this was the cause of my anger at Pimpi's letter the next morning. And I remind you of what you told me an hour ago: that if you had slept with Flinsparker it would be too late to do *our* love. Because then everything would be ruined. Or something along those lines. Roughly. Damn it all! *I* fell under this spell to a somewhat lesser degree and only for fifteen minutes. And paid for it with childish tantrums. Though that's more than enough to implicate myself in everything I say . . . Eh OK, the final result is: our deal is the same, but we have become different."

Bichette, having listened attentively with slightly bowed head, made a few small awkward gestures. "Do you admit that everything you do is stupid?"

Fec nodded hesitantly and contemptuously, at least just to acknowledge the significance of this resolution for himself.

Suddenly Bichette was standing in his way. "Does it make any difference *what* stupid things someone does, eh?"

"No. It's not like that." Fec's voice became uncertain, conscious of the dangerous turn the conversation was taking, but also under the glare of Bichette's scornful eyes. "Before we made our deal we were just idling and couldn't do it anymore. After we made our deal, which included nothing particularly special, we believed we would be on idle no more. But we ran around doing stupid things, even more on idle than before. We would've had to limit ourselves solely to work, being completely on idle, so as, under the terms of our deal, not to be on idle. Because there's only one remedy against the inevitability of being on idle: full awareness of being on idle."

"Sssss, slack that is!" Bichette's face tensed up impatiently. "That seems to me like . . . like — versifying. Bing, one is *always* fooling oneself. No matter the circumstances. Else it won't work at all. Else it's better just to turn the corner. Or go into the sweet air, as Monsieur Baron so nicely put it."

The fact that Bichette was standing still, almost unbearable at that moment, so excited Fec that he grabbed her hands, squeezed them tightly, and said, with great effort: "We're always, no matter the circumstances, fooling ourselves, of course. We always end up with the tralala. It's *impossible* to stay sharp. We've also just kidded ourselves about our deal. So it, too, should be canceled. But if it is canceled, our last opportunity goes with it. What remains is — nothingness. Or — the sweet air."

Bichette, giggling against all expectations, raised his hands and pressed them to her breasts. "Fec, I don't think our stupidities were all that stupid. As long as you still want to be here, it doesn't really matter what you do. The stuff we did wasn't the most atrociously stupid at all. Without it we would've been incredibly bored and wouldn't have the . . . élan to do what we've been doing. I mean Flinsparker. We're doing that one *now*. And *how!*"

Fec smiled, somehow relieved, almost glad. "Yes, in the end there's another, more amusing choice: either into the sweet air . . . or — straight on. Blind, wild, empty."

Bichette pulled him close, kissing the tip of his nose. "That 'or' is not correct. That 'or' can also be whatever you want it to be. For example — absolutely, *absolutely* wacko. Only the scams have to work. And they *will* work."

"I have a feeling only now we're . . ."

Bichette covered his mouth. "Only now will we have that final élan. Only now will things really start cooking." She spoke into his kisses. "Yes, you scamp, you sweet . . . Now we're gonna cook . . . Only now will it be really riche . . ."

Confused by this sudden ecstasy, Fec grew passive and brusquely pulled away. Then he stood there pensively.

But Bichette grabbed the front of his jacket and yanked it back and forth, laughing. "Just no more versifying, if I you please, eh?"

Fec felt quite silly. "No, no." He started to dance around on the grass with Bichette. "Ah, I see a thousand new possibilities. It's that old Great Game. And it's a high-stakes venture. But ours are higher, Bichon. The highest of all. That is, none at all. None at all."

"It seems to me you need this picked-up stuff for your own well-being . . . for your . . ." Bichette paused, alarmed.

"Yes, because I . . ."

"Shut your trap!" Bichette slapped her hand hard over his lips. So hard she bit into her thumb from the searing pain.

Fec snatched it and pressed it between his teeth, sucking on it with an indescribable smile.

And Bichette also began to smile in the same way . . .

They turned back. Anyone who saw them would believe they were a happy couple in love.

X

In the afternoon Laugier again waited in vain on the quay. For two hours.

In a state of agitation, he then made his way to Hotel Ruhl where Fec, acting on a spontaneous impulse, told him, now completely beside himself, that Bichette just phoned from Monte Carlo that Flinsparker had kidnapped her in his car and she was desperate . . .

Laugier gnashed his teeth. And he shuddered upon hearing that Bichette had sent him her regards, sharing his concern that Flinsparker's destination might be America.

"Let's go!" cried Laugier, lips trembling.

Fec tugged at his hair. "Right now! Ah it's always like this. Always. Ah . . ."

"What is?" Laugier spluttered.

"Eh OK, I only have ten francs. I've been waiting for a transfer for two days."

"Voilà." Laugier tossed his wallet on the table. "Three thousand francs! A little more. Go get Madame! At once! And come straight back! If you need more money, phone me!"

"But . . ." Fec hesitated in surprise.

"Yes, what else?!" Laugier's voice cracked hoarsely. "Why are you dawdling? How can you even hesitate? Man up! Punschoff!"

Fec turned his head and wrung his fingers: he thought it worthwhile to make it difficult for Laugier.

"Mon cher Baron." Laugier jovially slipped his arm around his shoulders. "An unfortunate, violated woman is appealing for help. I wouldn't act any differently if it were anyone else. And . . . are you not my friend?"

Fec narrowed his eyes tight and shook Laugier's hands vigorously.

"I've been here three times this morning." Laugier took his hat off the chair, tactfully distracting him. "I wanted to warn you. About Flinsparker. 'Tomorrow I'll have that wildcat!' He said that publicly. I also wanted to warn you about Watt-Wayler. He's furious. I promise you not to let him out of my sight, I will . . . Wait, maybe it would be better if I came with you . . ."

Fec raised his hands imploringly. "Just think about it . . ."

Laugier, like Fec, had no idea what there was to think about, and was instantly satisfied. "Ah, naturellement . . . alors bonne chance, mon cher Baron."

Fec shook his hand once again, and was off.

•

After five kilometers, Fec told the chauffeur to turn around and drive back to the hotel, and he had the suitcases, which were already packed, save a few small items, taken to the train station.

He arrived in Monte Carlo by evening, checked into the Hotel de Paris, and wrote the number of his room in red chalk (the signal of his arrival they had agreed upon) on the corner of the door of Flinsparker's suite.

At half past ten, Bichette appeared, completely unexpectedly, at Fec's door, threw her arms around his neck, and in a muffled squeal: "Fec, Fec, it's all working! It's all working!"

"How mindless!" Fec struggled to calm her.

"Bah. It's just the élan!"

"I do hope — the final."

Bichette clung tenderly to his shoulders. "And where will we go when it's over?"

"Florence."

"Richissimo!" After a kiss that lasted about two minutes, Bichette, quickly tore herself away and ran to the door. But abruptly paused, the handle in her hand, stared hard at Fec for a few seconds, and then lowered her head.

Somewhat reluctant and a little perplexed, Fec looked away. When he looked again, Bichette was gone.

•

Fec went to bed but couldn't sleep. A thousand things were running through his head. He felt as if he were spinning around himself. He could hardly see himself. Much less Bichette, whose relationship to him he was unable to fully fathom. He finally realized this was the real cause of his unease when he noticed how Bichette's piercing gaze, the one shortly before she had left him, returned to him with tormenting frequency without his being able to explain it. To make it easier, he forced himself to remember certain scenes, certain conversations, but they clarified nothing. Everything all at once seemed a muddle to him. Despite everything. Again and again, when a chain of thoughts unrolled before him, he tried, lifting his head, to see Bichette from within, as it were. Again and again, to no avail. He finally grinned at himself and suddenly said aloud, "Why can't I? . . . Ha, because I wouldn't find anything but her photograph."

He was so pleased with this extravagance that he became almost cheerful. The unease subsided. A gentle, comfortable indifference suffused through him. He smiled and stretched his body. When he was about to fall asleep, there was a faint knock.

He sprang out of bed and opened the door carefully.

Bichette slithered through it. "It's me."

Before Fec could say anything, she put two fingers in his mouth and toyed with his tongue.

Fec broke off angrily. "Are you out of your mind! If someone sees you!"

"But nobody *saw* me."

"The hallways of big hotels like this are always watched at night. What if Flinsparker wakes up? What then . . ."

"*He* won't wake up. Oh, what a halfwit! He's nice though. Very nice actually." Bichette looked at a small picture on the wall.

Fec had to smile. "Are you trying to make me jealous?"

"I hope you're kidding."

Fec was amazed she could doubt it and warily kept his eyes on her.

Bichette noticed and ran her hands through his hair. "Fec, tell me, do you love me?" She stuck out her tongue, meant to be self-deprecating, or so it seemed, but came off as merely repugnant.

"To the point of insensibility," whispered Fec, a deliberate act, and he politely kissed Bichette's bare neck.

At that moment he somehow sensed, smelled, saw, tasted what had happened between Flinsparker and Bichette before she had entered his room. He was seized by a familiar excitation, one that had always been incomprehensible to him yet nonetheless enthralled him anew. His breathing became irregular and intermittent. His lips trembled on Bichette's back.

"That, I can put up with." Bichette had no doubt he was pretending, and breathed angrily: "But why the reticence? Might Monsieur Baron demur because . . ."

Fec's senses reeled. "Yes, yes, yes, yes . . . and what else . . ." He assaulted Bichette's mouth with his own, felt it still hot from the other man, a quick burning pang ran through him before fading into a subtle, distant rage that his breath, gone and then returning heavy and broken, thrust into a savage bite.

Bichette emitted a voluptuous gurgle. Then, feeling blood run warmly over her skin, she moaned, closed her eyes, and greedily opened her mouth wide . . .

Fec stammered something. His left leg wobbled a little and made him teeter. He then grabbed Bichette and threw her under him . . .

•

". . . you're telling me for the third time now. I'll do it just like that. Exactly like that." Bichette got up from the bidet. "But . . ." She dried herself carefully with both hands. "But do you know why I asked if you love me?"

Fec shrugged indifferently.

"Just to see if it still bothers you."

Fec's lips moved mockingly.

"You weren't upset, were you? Or maybe?"

Fec rubbed his hands.

"Fec!" When she saw his eyes again, Bichette rested her own on his naked body. "Do you call *this* kidding *too?*"

Fec grabbed the covers and lay back on the pillows.

Bichette ran to the bed and turned her shoulder with the bite wound before Fec's eyes. "And what about *this,* huh?"

"That was . . ." Fec paused for a long time, lips parted, "I don't know yet."

"May I ask you, Monsieur Baron, to please inform me as soon as you . . ." Bichette jumped into bed with both knees.

"You may."

"Merci." Bichette salivated onto two fingers and rubbed the spit on the wound. "What if Flinsparker sees the bite?"

"You'll tell him something."

"Fec!"

"What?"

"Don't you know?"

"What!"

"Why you bit me."

"No." Incapable of anything more, Fec pulled the covers up to his forehead.

"Fec!" Bichette yanked them off him.

"What the hell!" Fec sat up angrily.

"Bing, how's that for a venture?" Without looking at him, Bichette tied the silk ribbons on her blouse she had taken from the chair.

Fec reached for a cigarette.

"Fec, listen!"

"What is it?"

"This thing with the venture."

"What venture?"

"Not the one on my blouse." Bichette giggled confidently. "But the one that isn't one. And the money? Is that not a venture, eh?"

Fec smoked in amusement. "So, you assume I might actually believe what I choose to say." He was eager to hear her reply.

Bichette sat down weightily. "You won't evade me like this. The money *is* a venture. If *that* isn't a venture either, then you've stupidly contradicted yourself." She began to tidy her hair, firmly convinced she had caused him a great deal of anguish.

Fec gnawed at his cigarette, smiled, and tossed it into a corner. Then he gently slapped his thigh with the palm of his hand and quietly sang the chorus of a popular Parisian song with lyrics he added himself: "Rien que sa photo."

"Fec, something like that could happen to *you?*" Bichette kicked at him.

Suddenly it all became too much for Fec. "And now please leave at once!" He wanted to take her hand and pull her out of bed.

But Bichette deftly threw herself next to him. "Not so fast. I want an answer." She rubbed her body against his, exerting maximum pressure. "Don't worry, by the way! The guy over there is sleeping like a log."

Fec gave in so as not to appear afraid.

"So, how is it?"

Fec pushed her belly away, gathering what strength he could: he would manage somehow.

Bichette's knee nudged him on the hip. "Well . . . ?"

Without yet knowing what he wanted to say, Fec began hesitantly: "Our venture consists of two parts . . . but together essentially form an integral whole. The first part is . . . : we pass the time, chasing large sums of money as best we can . . . as long as we don't have enough yet to pass the time with a pension . . . The second part is . . . : working, we spend less now than our future pension will have to be . . . because, not working, we will have to spend far more in order not to get bored . . . Eh OK, do you understand?"

Bichette raised a dubious eye.

Fec spoke as if he were blind. "Of course, this venture is purely negative. Yet safeguarding ourselves from work and boredom is not a venture. The real venture is our very life. The fact that we ourselves belong, above all, to our avocations. The body gives what it has to give. Its pleasures are real. You can't fool yourself about that . . . Of course, in the end, to live is not a venture. But we don't want to hang ourselves. So, in spite of everything, we have no venture. Because we'll always be living pointlessly. In a way that provides us with the most fun, the most pleasure."

Bichette hadn't moved, and kept staring at Fec, unblinking. Now she averted her eyes, laughing. "Fec, you're versifying again. You're nutso, Fec."

"Shut it!" Fec's eyes became small. "Maybe I'm just a figment of my own imagination." But no sooner did he say it than he had to crack a smile.

Bichette slapped him on the butt. "No, you're my sweet scamp . . . my sweet scamp . . ."

This term of endearment, which had almost always

somewhat befuddled him, now stirred him inside. With every fiber of his being he searched for a distraction. "Have you answered Pimpi yet?"

Bichette lay there with her hands under her neck, her legs over Fec's. "What should I write to him?"

"Now please tell me what you had with Ralix."

Bichette grumpily clamped her lower lip between her teeth. "I don't really feel like it . . . But given everything . . . It was a real hive of hoods in the Royal Bar. You know the joint, it's on Rue Fontaine. I went, and I have no idea why, up there with him. With Harry, who likes to act all posh, the child. But it was over with Harry long ago. Couci-couça, and once upstairs I immediately get pulled over to a table. And then this fat fuckface wanted to drag me into his car on the street. Harry had disappeared. Must have rolled someone. Suddenly Ralix was standing there. Probably waiting for Loute, who was working the Royal at the time. Well, Ralix just said to the pig: 'Please unhand Madame!' That alone did the trick. Because the ole boy has that look! Like a zebra. You know it, don't you? So he shacked up with me. It lasted about a week. Then I got sick of him. But he wasn't sick of me just yet. He also had the horrible habit of singing in bed. Not like you, well, maybe a little. But loudly, and every five minutes, and the dumbest operas. But mainly he was too much a wack job for me. I mean, he's very sly and has enough courage for three, but for me, there was just something missing with him. The thing that's always missing. There's always something missing, eh? Well, I couldn't get rid of him at all. Insults, abuse, kicking — nothing worked. One time I spat in his face in front of everyone on the terrace of Le Cyrano. He just swallowed the saliva and grinned. There was simply nothing I could do. And I was already sick of all the yak! So at that point I had to cut the bait on this last chump and sent Tall Georges, the cop who always stands at the corner of Rue Blanche, a chilly look and I slipped a few tidbits into his hand in the next-door entranceway, and four days later they busted my Ralix . . . Bing."

Fec cleared his throat, slowly lifting his head. "Does anyone know?"

Bichette thought about it. "Maybe Pimpi, he heard me threaten this once before in one of my rages. But Ralix doesn't know. And I can rely on Tall Georges. Ralix might suspect it. In any case, he doesn't know for certain. Because the other two who got nicked because of me did some stupid bullshit. They thought they could keep me with a lot of money, the arrogant mooks. And Ralix knows about that as does everyone else." As Fec stared at the wall in silence, Bichette brought several items from the bathroom to the bed and began to comb her armpit hair forward so that short strands of hair were visible. "It's my invention. They all love it. And to think some ninnies actually shave it?" She scowled, irritated by Fec's silence. "Got a problem?"

Fec had come up with one explanation after another for her story, which struck him as implausible. Since none quite satisfied him, he asked, almost imperiously: "What can keep you down?"

Bichette whistled softly so as to leave her face expressionless. "You."

Fec coughed, convinced she meant to annoy him. "So, there's nothing missing with me? All there? All there?"

Bichette wrapped her arms around her knees, pulled them to her chest, and rocked. "All there! All there!"

"Splendid!" Fec laughed.

"Rotter!"

After a long pause, during which Bichette trimmed her toenails, Fec, who had lit another cigarette, said abruptly: "Nothing's there. Everything's missing between us."

Bichette continued trimming with undivided attention. "Everything's missing. Why not?"

"*That's* how to keep you down: — with nothing."

Bichette finally seemed to have finished her pedicure. "With nothing?" She looked at each toe in turn. "What're you talking about? With nothing? How's that?"

Fec had the impression Bichette had more than understood him and was shocked he still felt the need to speak. "With nothing, that is — with utmost sincerity. By telling you that *even* this could be a con. And that would be the best. But that you also have to make do without it because . . ."

Bichette was now listening intently, ". . . because . . ."

Suddenly everything became so unbearable to Fec that he just kept talking because he felt it would become even more unbearable if he didn't, ". . . because this renunciation is one of the greatest delights . . . perhaps the greatest of all. But it means not succumbing to the suggestion of money. And since pleasure, in any form, is only a variety of suggestion, it's so easy to get taken in by surprise. Suggestion is just power, energy. Suggestion is life itself. But one mustn't succumb to life in any of its many forms. Renunciation is the most profound, most sublime pleasure."

Bichette placed her hands lightly over her eyes. "You said

earlier that the pleasures of the body are real, you can't fool yourself. And now you're saying they're just 'suggestion.' Another stupid contradiction."

"Suggestion is life itself," said Fec, stubbornly and wearily.

Bichette moved on to her manicure. "Maybe."

Fec brought the cigarette he had forgotten about to his lips. As he slowly blew smoke in front of him, he thought aloud, "Yes, our deal is a renunciation."

"And a pleasure."

Fec's chin twitched in surprise. He suddenly realized it was distrust that made him speak. So he said sharply: "Even so, you're not really safe. No one's safe. A whim, a downpour, a woman, a bad cigarette, devil knows what it might be — and now renunciation of renunciation is experienced as the highest pleasure and that's that — the other's been rolled pathetically."

Bichette dropped the scissors. "Anything goes." She put her fingers on top of one another. "*Anything.*"

"That's why you can't get involved in anything. Nothing at *all.*" Fec smiled at the contradiction between his words and his situation. And he almost scoffed when he added, "For me, *everyone* is my bitterest enemy. Everyone. Everyone. Everyone."

Bichette glanced to the side. The pinkies of each hand moved a little upward. "Me too?"

Seconds passed before Fec said in a firm voice, more out of an indomitable curiosity than because he really believed it, "You too." He put down the cigarette.

Bichette slowly moved up to him and put her arm behind his neck. The nails of her other hand dug into his thigh, forcing him down on the bed with her body. Then she opened her lips in front of his, sucked in his breath, gave him hers, and stared between his brow wide-eyed.

It seemed to Fec as if she wanted to kill him with her breath. As he thought it, he had to clench his teeth to keep from smiling.

Then Bichette pinched his cheek briefly and breathed: "Fec, you're a dipshnuk."

He didn't know what she meant. But at that moment this was preferable, as he was so filled with an intense, rare pleasure.

•

When Bichette had gotten dressed, Fec heard the hour strike five. He vaguely noticed she had come to him both times in flats. As he gently pushed the bolt back, Bichette asked softly: "So nothing's changed?"

"Naturally. You hung it in the fireplace, didn't you?"

"Yes."

Fec, thinking of the previous conversation, pursed his lips in doubt. "It's not that much actually. How much did you say . . . ?"

"I couldn't count it." Bichette looked at her feet. "Barely less than fifteen thousand."

"Why don't you put it in the vase in the hallway for now instead."

Bichette nodded without looking up.

"And do it quickly! Preferably while leaning over the balustrade for a moment, as if you've noticed something. But you have to really make sure you have to go to the toilet, no matter what. Even if you don't see anyone."

Bichette nodded hastily several times, stepping from one foot to the other.

"So at eight o'clock. And don't forget to leave the door unlocked. Au revoir."

Bichette waved her hand awkwardly as she slipped out.

•

At eight o'clock that morning Fec stormed into Flinsparker's bedroom, pistol in hand, pulled Bichette, who was screaming pitifully, out of bed and roared: "You shall be hearing from me again soon!"

Flinsparker, drowsily trying to sit up on the pillows, barely had time to express astonishment. He only understood the connection later when he was alone for a while.

When the staff appeared in the hallway, startled by the screaming, they found it already empty and only a few sleepy, inquiring faces in some doorways.

Flinsparker had his suspicions of Fec already in Nice. This is why he preferred to avoid any scandal, which inevitably would have been rather embarrassing for him. After an hour he sent Fec a check for ten thousand francs through his chauffeur, since if he was refused, he would only risk having to avoid the Riviera for the rest of the season.

Fec received the note with the check as he was giving some instructions in the porter's lodge. Ten minutes later he left the hotel with Bichette in tow.

They drove to Menton, where Fec cashed the check.

XI

The next day, very early in the morning, Bichette asked Fec to get a certain toiletry item for her.

When he returned to the hotel from this errand, during which he had remembered to wire Laugier for money, he was informed, not without a hint of derision, that Madame Thaller had left for the train station with her suitcases half an hour ago.

Fec looked at his watch, more amazed at how calmly he received this news more than the news itself. It was nine o'clock. The train to Genoa, which he had planned to take with Bichette, was leaving an hour later. There could be no doubt: Bichette had taken the express to Paris.

Fec entered his room very slowly. His eyes darted from one object to the other: no letter, no note.

His two suitcases stood in a corner.

He sat down on the largest one, took a cigarette, and was no longer even surprised that he was not surprised. Although he hadn't allowed himself to be conscious of it, the possibility existed all along that Bichette might leave him, as she had done with all his predecessors. And he remembered that in Monte Carlo, the night before their sting, as soon as Bichette had gone out the door, he repeated her words, "You're a — dipshnuk" to himself in a low voice and had the feeling he had heard something crucial. Now he felt as if he had already known then that Bichette would leave him. Even him.

He smiled glumly, even in boredom. So was this the end? His last adventure? He knew it would end like all adventures. After all that had gone before, he thought it banal that Bichette had taken not only her jewelry, but also all the money, and grotesque that she had left surreptitiously.

He suddenly got up. Thinking of particular conversations, Bichette's uninhibited tendency to play the vagabond, her innate cruelty and wickedness struck him as ridiculous explanations, so ridiculous that his mistrust, otherwise always prepared for the end result, but which had admittedly become diminished with Bichette, now surged: this departure might well be a clever gambit, an outstanding ruse . . .

And now he was already clutching his temples and grinning. "No, it's nothing like that. I just don't *want* it to be true. I *want* my last adventure. I *want* a different ending . . ."

He also didn't want to be the one deserted, the one who lost, which he again refused to allow himself to accept. He wanted it to end the way he wanted it to. Yes, so how did he want it to end? What did he want?

He paced the room with long strides. A dull, pounding fury overtook him. At breakneck speed he replayed all the conversations with Bichette, every word he had found striking, every gesture that had aroused him, everything left unsaid, all the confusion, all the tenderness, all the crassness, in short, *all* of it again passed before his eyes.

At last he stopped, slapped his hand on his forehead and muttered: "And I find nothing but my photograph. Nothing else. What do I want now? Am I an idiot? I-di-ot?"

After about five minutes, an idiotic expression actually did come over his face.

It was only when the room waiter brought him Laugier's telegram with the requested three thousand francs did everything fall together: the fact was that without this money he would have only had one hundred and fifty francs to his name.

"Order me a fast tourer to Paris right away!" He wanted to be sitting in the Léon when Bichette came in, he wanted to see her eyes when she saw him, he wanted . . .

•

The car passed Porte de Vincennes around ten at night.

At ten-fifteen it stopped on Rue l'Ecluse, a side street off Boulevard des Batignolles, in front of the little Hotel de l'Europe.

And at a quarter to eleven Fec appeared in the Léon.

He scanned the whole place with a single glance. He saw not one familiar face. Not even Jean was there.

When Fec stepped out into the street to hail a taxi, his hand abruptly stopped its motion: for some strange reason he only now thought of Ralix. There was a good chance this man was connected to Bichette's departure. Pimpi might have warned her. Maybe Paris wasn't the play at all, but . . . It was not so easy to work out an angle that made sense. The most likely scenario would be that Bichette was, in fact, in Paris. So Fec gave up wracking his brains for any other ideas, all the more since he hoped to learn everything he needed from Pimpi.

He had the taxi stop in front of Hotel Fécamp on Place de Budapest.

Pimpi lived on the fifth floor. Although the doorman said Monsieur Pimpi was not at home, Fec climbed the five steep flights of stairs. On the way, on a landing, he felt slightly dizzy from his hurry. To avoid staggering against the wall, he grabbed an old, moth-eaten curtain, which coated him in clouds of dust.

He finally reached Pimpi's door and paused, out of breath. His impatience, which he cursed and yet felt growing by the minute, made him wonder if it might not be wiser to put the visit off.

But by then he'd already knocked.

Listening feverishly, he grimaced in some distress at the sour smell of dust and dishwater.

Someone shuffled inside to the door, fiddled with it for a moment, mumbled something, and finally slowly opened it a crack.

Pimpi's gaunt, wrinkled face appeared in the door crack. His pomaded hair was partly pushed back from the forehead and partly standing stiffly.

"Good day, Pimpi. How are you?" The tone of Fec's voice was so off he wondered whether it might not be wiser to use some pretext to say goodbye.

"Back from the woods so soon?" Pimpi rubbed his stubble and stopped wagging his head. "And no pretty lass, yo?"

"Have you . . . Have you, by chance, seen Gaby the past few days?" Delighted he hadn't given himself away, Fec became talkative. "I was told half an hour ago that she . . ." He spoke for about five minutes before Pimpi found the opportunity to tell him that Gaby had recently broken both legs by falling out of a window but her life wasn't in danger.

"Yo. You sure spiffy!" Pimpi interrupted Fec, who had just started talking. "Where you get those duds?"

"We were in Nice." Fec looked past Pimpi, bewildered at himself.

"Yo, yo," Pimpi laughed in his amiable way, albeit with an unmistakable absence of certainty, which Fec nevertheless failed to pick up on due to his own nervousness. "But your face . . . Looks caved in."

"Caved in . . . how?" repeated Fec in surprise. It was obvious, though, that he'd replied heedlessly. Then he smiled quickly. "It was not a pleasant trip."

Pimpi creaked the door, still holding it in his hand. "Why'd you come back? Dusty trip?" He patted the dust off his clothes, trying to be jovial.

Fec's forehead twitched briefly: something about Pimpi's behavior seemed odd to him. So much so that he finally gave up his original intention to confide in him, which he had nearly recklessly done at the outset, having stopped just short. He replied as calmly as he could: "Eh OK, you know what I had with Gaby. I'd like to know where she is."

"Where she . . . Yo, in Lariboisière Hospital."

Suddenly Fec had the bizarre idea that Bichette might have already visited Gaby, and he hastily said goodbye.

"What's with you?" Pimpi made a funny face. "Where's Bichette?" His ears quivered slightly.

"I have a taxi waiting downstairs." Fec rushed to the stairs, angry he hadn't known how to lie.

"And I haven't a penny." Pimpi put his index fingers to his ears and whimpered comically.

Fec tossed him a banknote, the first he got his hands on, and ran down the stairs.

Pimpi's Negro laugh echoed behind him.

•

At the hospital, Fec had a hard time getting in to see Gaby, and only managed it with twenty francs.

She was so surprised and moved by the unexpected visit that tears welled in her eyes.

On the nightstand beside her bed stood a glass with freesias.

Fec noticed it right off and asked impetuously, thinking of Bichette: "Who brought you the flowers?"

Gaby's eyes widened with joy. "Nurse Madelon . . . Who did you think?"

"When will you be up and about?" Fec asked this even dumber question just to cover up his first dumb question and angrily held his throat.

Gaby's shoulder edged forward.

"I never seem to fall right either." She smirked glumly. One bloodless hand poked in her hair and the other timidly stroked Fec's knee. "Lovely suit."

Fec saw the scar from Bichette's bite and instinctively lowered his head.

Seeing this, Gaby took his hand. "So you too, she . . ." She didn't dare finish the sentence. Then she said softly, "She's a magnificent creature. But I don't think that she . . ."

Fec waited a little before pressing: "... that she ..."

"Anyway, thank you so much for coming. You're the only one. You're the only one at all." Gaby buried her face in the pillow and began to sob.

While Fec caressed her mechanically, he debated whether it was appropriate to question her. But his curiosity got the best of him. "Have you seen Ralix?"

"Fec!" Gaby shouted suddenly and sat up straight. "I, Fec, I ..." She stammered. Her shimmering whitish eyes rounded like a fish. She gasped: "*I* brought that Japanese guy into it, I ... Oh, I was ... Leave me alone! Just leave me alone! Go on! Go to her, you ... you ... Don't mind me, you jackass ... you jackass ... Oh, it's stupid, eh? So fucking stupid ..."

Since some of the patients in the room had woken up and become restless, Fec clasped Gaby with both arms and slowly forced her back into bed.

When she was lying down again, she put her hands around his neck, pressed her cheek to his, and whispered in his ear in a shaky voice amid laughter and sobs: "Oh, Fec, I would love you so much, *so* much ... I would even leave the Coco if you wanted me to. I know you don't like it ... Oh, I was beside myself with fear at the time that something might happen to you. But I swear to you it wasn't me. I didn't know anything about that Japanese guy. But when Jean let go of me after Bichette bit my hand ... I ran out into the street but didn't see you anywhere. I ran around like crazy, through a few cafés, and then on Rue Véron I ran into Loute, who could see right away that something was wrong with me and took me away and asked me what's up, and ditz that I am I tell her everything and cry and rant and make threats and . . . Loute hates Bichette intensely because she was jilted by Ralix when he took up with her and because she knows it was Bichette that got Ralix pinched. Now I don't believe it. She doesn't do things like *that* . . . Oh, you asked me about Ralix. I don't know if he's out yet. But if he's out, then she should watch her back. Because Loute is sure to tell him it was Bichette, and then . . . Fec, I'm telling you something I wouldn't be telling you if I were like the others. I'm telling you to warn Bichette. And that's why I'm also telling you not to . . . Leave her be! She's pulled the wool over *everyone's* eyes. Oh, Fec. I'd do anything you want. By the way, did you know Pimpi's her confidant? She must have some special bond with him. Because they're always seen together . . . Fec, I would hustle for you, if you wanted me to, I would . . . Oh, Fec . . . Please believe me, I swear it was Loute. That lanky-assed bitch just took advantage of me in my agitated state and dragged me into a café where the Japanese guy was sitting and spilled the beans about everything. I didn't open my mouth there at all. But when that horrible man suddenly took off, I had a bad feeling about it and wanted to tell you. I ran around all day. Where were you? Only the next day I found out from Jean how you flattened the Japanese and wanted . . . Where were you? It drove me crazy that I couldn't find you . . . Oh, that made me . . ." Her chest heaved. She could no longer speak for the sobbing.

After expending a good deal of effort to calm her down, Fec left her to the nurse, who had come in to finally put an end to the night's visit.

•

Fec took a taxi to his hotel, washed and changed clothes, and walked down the street aimlessly.

After a few steps he turned around, hurried back to his room, and exchanged his elegant cutaway for his old gray suit and dark green scarf. It annoyed him to have to take the coat so as not to arouse the manager's suspicion.

He spent the rest of the night in small bistros with familiar cocottes. Neither here nor anywhere else was he able to find out a thing about Bichette, nor if Ralix had been seen.

At about six in the morning, completely soused, he went back to the Léon. Jean was there and greeted him exuberantly. But he didn't know anything either.

Leaning against a house on Place Blanche later, his wet lips pressed together in determined rage, Fec decided not to think anymore about the reason for Bichette's departure or about her possible whereabouts, but simply to look for her. Everywhere. For days. For weeks. He would find her. Whatever the circumstances. He *must* find her. This self-imposed "must" became his purpose and gave his life meaning.

XII

The visit to Gaby had firmly convinced Fec, without his really knowing why, that Bichette was in Paris. Day and night he roamed the streets, through restaurants, cafés, bars, and dance halls. He neglected no quarter and no bistro. He inquired everywhere, in detail. He also frequented the upscale restaurants and tea rooms.

He led this sort of life for about three weeks. He ran into Pimpi once, tried to cautiously sound him out, but only received replies that left him doubting if Pimpi really knew anything at all. He visited Gaby several times in the hospital without being able to learn anything useful; a motley of new tales, feverishly told and no doubt partly invented, had so blurred the impression left by the first visit that Fec gave up trying to run into Loute. The only thing he had to go on came from Jean, who told him he had seen Ralix twice, walking through the café, apparently looking for someone, and once in the company of a woman. From the description, Fec suspected it was Loute.

That same evening, he saw her standing on the corner of Rue Caulaincourt, in front of a poster for Gaumont Palace. He approached her.

Loute, who knew him only by sight, was not at all

surprised, and in fact acted as if she were speaking to an old friend.

She asked Fec to accompany her to a house on Rue Lamarck. They talked the whole way, cheerfully, often outdoing each other for seconds at a time in pleasantries, funny ideas, and wild exaggerations.

While Fec was waiting for Loute in front of the house, it occurred to him that her behavior might be motivated by the same intention as his, to conceal some specific interest. He decided he should be careful.

Loute skipped out of the house laughing, clung to Fec's arm and, in an effervescent mood and chattering nonstop, dragged him into a small café.

After a few minutes there, one of those excruciating pauses arose quite suddenly and without either of them being able to prevent it, which often can ruin everything and reveal much.

Loute seemed to sense this as well. She deliberately avoided Fec's gaze, busied herself with her Picon, and finally began to make conversation in the most primitive manner.

When Fec wanted to say goodbye later on the street, irritated by his lack of success, Loute asked that he go with her to the Elysée Montmartre. Fec was about to refuse, but gladly agreed as he suspected she was pursuing a particular agenda. While she was dancing, he observed her discreetly, but without noticing anything special. And when she showed no surprise that he didn't ask her to dance, nor even an oblique gesture to suggest surprise, he was convinced she was not trying to play him off against Ralix, whom he believed was present in the dance hall.

Around eleven o'clock Loute suggested they leave, but pop into Liberty's Bar for another drink. Fec agreed, if only with a measure of resignation.

When they entered, all heads turned to them even more conspicuously than was normal.

Having sat down and ordered, Fec looked around with a keen eye. And suddenly, directly in front of him, separated only by the small square dance floor, he saw Bichette.

She was sitting between two middle-aged gentlemen, laughing and joking, and although she must have noticed Fec long beforehand, she didn't alter her demeanor in the least.

Fec was amazed that the unexpected sight of Bichette did not upset him. He continued to chat with Loute, who appeared not to attach any importance to the encounter, as he mulled off and on just what course of action would be the smartest. He finally decided, when he saw Bichette dancing, to ask her to a one-step, a dance that offered the best opportunity for conversation.

Bichette stood up politely when he came over to her table and, as if he were the first to come to her, raised her elbows with charming nonchalance.

Fec embraced her with utmost reserve and after a few bars said calmly: "I'd like to speak with you alone today."

Bichette looked dispassionately at his shoulder. "Will be difficult."

"Why did you leave?" Fec's voice quavered.

Bichette laughed under her breath. "Bah. I didn't give it a second thought."

Fec, immediately aware of the double mockery of these words, stared at a spot just below her ear, seeing poorly powdered bluish marks on her throat and back of her neck, which must have been caused by an assault. For a moment he thought of Ralix. "Did he mess you up like that?"

"He . . . ? Who?"

"Ralix."

"Mess . . . me up?"

"The bruises."

"Sssss . . . What's it to you, eh?"

"So, it was Ralix."

"Oh, you don't know me very well." Bichette turned her head and directed a churlish smile at the gentlemen at her table.

"Eh OK. Tell me when and where I can speak with you."

Bichette was silent for a long time. "Come here tomorrow afternoon around five."

"You won't be here."

"Fraid? Nah, not me."

"So that's that."

"And tell Loute she's resourceful."

"Resourceful . . . ?"

Bichette left him standing there.

•

Lying in bed, Fec kept thinking about why Loute might have brought him to Bichette, and why she smiled so maliciously when he asked her about it. The most likely explanation was that she had wanted to wound Bichette's pride and at the same time discover how she felt about him. Yet this was contradicted by the fact that Loute refused to dance with him and had gone to the restroom while he was dancing with Bichette.

The thought of the impending confrontation, about which Fec had no doubt, ultimately pushed everything else aside. He considered it from every angle. And after three hours he came to the rather surprising conclusion that in the end he was completely indifferent to the outcome. The only thing important to him was that he would have the opportunity to speak to Bichette one more time and that he would be the first to leave.

His morning was nonetheless spent completely in the grip of unbearably agonizing expectation. His impatience had so gotten the best of him that by three o'clock that afternoon he was sitting by a window of Brasserie Graff, from where he had a view of almost the entire Place Blanche. Strangely enough it was here, during these unnerving two hours, that connections he had been blind to, situations that had remained a mystery to him, now became clear, and only now did he grasp the true meaning of certain words. Yet he managed to stay in place until ten minutes past five.

When Fec was about four steps from the bar's entrance, he saw Bichette approaching from Rue Blanche. He immediately noticed how fastidiously she had dressed, almost more elegantly than in Nice, but wearing no jewelry.

"Don't have the slightest desire to sit in there." Bichette didn't even offer her hand. "Let's walk . . . if that's okay with you."

"I believe you, you're not afraid . . . Eh OK, let's go."

They turned in silence onto Boulevard de Clichy.

"I wanted to speak with you again," Fec finally began, his voice strained, "to ask why you left so suddenly."

"Knew it." Bichette's upper lip curled in disgust. "Not something I gave much thought to. I was just bored."

"I don't think so," annoyed, Fec shoved his nervous hands into his pockets, and was even more annoyed that he did. "You sure were pleased with our debut down there. And you were also quite pleased with the result. In Menton, you were outright giddy with glee. Not to mention in Cap-d'Ail, where you kissed that little bellhop! And how the chauffeur had to race on the way back! And how you screamed and cavorted! I'd never seen you like that before."

"Bah. You might as well relive the moments that made me fall madly in love with you."

Fec didn't bother to respond so as not to offend her pride. "So then, *what* exactly were you bored with?"

"You." Bichette tucked her thick parasol under her armpit and looked straight ahead, sullen.

"Why?"

"Because . . ." Bichette malevolently pursed her lips, ". . . because you're too fine a fellow. Or better — too fine a person. And as I told you right at the start, I consider such types pains in the ass."

Fec was astounded. "Me — a fine person?"

"Yes, you! I couldn't take all that smart-assed bullshit anymore. I liked you at the beginning when you kept your mouth shut. When you decked that Japanese oaf. When you embarrassed that ace of a cretin from Avenue des Ternes. And when you were drunk and made that terrific deal. And when we were leaving, after that crazy tralala in the taxi, you asked me to slap you. And when you were so delightfully cheeky down there. But I liked you best at the start, when you still kept your horrible mouth shut. And in bed of course. Though in the end *that* gets boring with anyone."

Fec was silent for several seconds, so taken aback by her words. Struggling, he finally managed: "You once said something very true . . . — that it's *all* stupid . . ."

"That's why everything works out. And that's why I'm surprised you're starting to bore me all over again. Why go on and on about me leaving? I *simply* left and basta! Or maybe that alone *won't* do the trick, eh?"

"Bichette!" Her name slipped out against his will. To avoid the appearance of giving ground, he asked as cheerfully as he could: "Tell me something else. Just before you went back to Flinsparker the night before our sting went down, you said I was a — dipshnuk . . . Why did you say that?"

Bichette, who up to now had spoken with cold scorn, laughed affectedly. "Oh . . . then . . . ?" She paused, as if making an effort to remember. "Then . . . ?" I meant that I was *always* your bitterest enemy."

"Ah." Fec had to smile. "Some of the time it sure didn't seem that way."

"Some of the time?" cried Bichette. "How about that! Yeah, many times, in fact! But what does that prove, huh? *What* won't we do to experience something new? What *won't* we do! We'd do *anything*, that's what."

Fec stopped, his cheeks flushed. His whole face contracted convulsively. There was a watery gleam in his eyes as he said softly, but with his voice clearly betraying delight: "I truly didn't expect *that* from you, Bichette. Not *that*. You are simply — masterful. Hats off!" And he actually doffed his cap and bowed to her.

"Merci." Bichette, barely concealing her satisfaction, played with the ivory handle of her parasol. "Even you have crying spells."

Fec's head snapped up. "*That,* I don't think so. *Not* that."

"I do."

Fec was suddenly having doubts, and he thought it wiser to give in to find out everything. "Possibly."

"Absolutely."

"Absolutely?" Fec smiled wanly, almost convinced.

"Absolutely!" Bichette walked slowly. "Bah. I'll help your memory. And maybe you as well."

"Help me?

"Yeah, by curing you of me. By revealing my secret. By telling . . ."

"Secret . . . ?"

"Yeah, secret! . . . By humbly telling you that from the start I had an exquisite intention, and it was to make you fall in love with me, you hear — in love! And then leave you. Bing, I'll tell you now that it wasn't a total success."

"Not total," said Fec calmly.

"Be patient, Monsieur Baron!" Bichette coughed with an air of superiority. "I started crying just to see what you would do next. I was masterful, eh? Didn't you fall for it hook, line, and sinker? It's all on you. Because you bought me that yellow wool cap. You took the three hundred francs. And you took the bait when I suggested we do us. I didn't imagine your lovely deal, but something like it. I wanted you to make the effort to fall in love with me, and then end up really being in love with me. In that sense, I was the one driving the bus. And that's the only reason I said at the time that you belong to me and me to you. Of course, I didn't like *your* deal. That's why I made that scene with my jewelry at Hotel Puget. Not because I was fickle. But because I couldn't take your delightful deal seriously for a single second. With this . . . this gesture of self-sacrifice, I wanted to bind you to me even more firmly, so that it would be even easier to make you fall in love with me. That's why I was so pleased when you hit me. The only reason you hit me then was because you were happy I gave myself up so completely, so completely . . . I screamed *only* to make you fall in love with me. *That's why* I asked you on the balcony at Hotel Ruhl what was up with you: not because I believed our love was showing, and not because I believed I was starting to bore you, but because for the first time I feared I might not be able to make you fall in love with me. *That's why* I got pissed when you copped that pimp attitude. Not the one I know so well and is entirely different and goes hand in hand with googly eyes and heart and . . . Rotter! . . . but that dry, matter-of-fact tone, it threw me after everything that already happened. And *that's why,* after our first evening working the Jetée, I ginned up that slack love scene that made me laugh even at myself. *That's why* I wired Pimpi to tell him to write. The letter from him worked. You were actually fuming about it and a little jealous. Ah, but only a little. *That's why* I broke character on the second work evening at the Jetée and flew off the handle. *That's why* I later confessed in the room that it was stronger than me, a success when you admitted to feeling something similar when you read Pimpi's letter. And *that's why* I was angry the next morning when I realized, after pretending to be asleep, that you might not be able to fall in love with me after all. And *that's why* I kicked Red Bia that same evening at the Jetée, but also out of anger because I didn't want to succeed. *That's why* the whole mad scene. And the result was you beat the crap out of Watt-Wayler. In the end it was just jealousy. And this is why later I was fully convinced you actually did love me when I said: 'We love each other.' But the next morning at breakfast, when you said the Flinsparker scam was still on, I felt I'd been wrong. And when we had that long, stupid conversation outside Cannes, I knew for sure I wouldn't succeed in making you fall in love with me. From that moment on I actually started to get bored. You started to bore me. The fact that I was happy at the end of that conversation was a con. At that point, I wanted to run away. I only stayed so I could choose the right moment for leaving that would give you the most to chew over. When it would seem totally implausible and inexplicable that I should take off. So this explains my high spirits in Menton and Cap-d'Ail. And do you know why, apparently for no reason, I suddenly came to your room in Monte Carlo? Just to see if you *might* want to change your mind about me sleeping with Flinsparker . . . And when I came to you again afterward, around three in the morning, again for no apparent reason, I only came to see if *now* you might think differently. But you weren't weak and meek like others, instead you were delighted about it. Or just pretended to be to get under my skin. But I also noticed during the conversation that followed for the first time you were more detached than usual, for the first time all your energy wasn't put into . . . couci-couça versifying, and for the first time you were almost indifferent. You didn't make the least effort to answer my wily questions even halfway cleverly. You acted this way *only* after I slept with someone else. This always happens. But with *you* it *shouldn't* have been like that. Not with *you*. You would have . . . Bing, do you know what would've kept me? You should have loved me and then left me. You — to me. Then I would've run after you and maybe torn you to shreds if you wouldn't stay with me. I thought you were the only man capable of running away from me. And you have to run away from me if you really love me. But you ran after me like everyone else. So I ran away from you when I knew for sure you would never run away from me. Never. And I knew it when you told me that I, too, was your bitterest enemy. Because a man only says something like that when he's trying to cleverly convince himself of the opposite. And I tell you again that I've always been your bitterest enemy. Because if I'd completely achieved all I wanted, you would have run away from me, rejected me, then I would've run after you, and that would've caused me to tear you to shreds . . . Bah! In any case, it would've been very bad for you . . . By the way, do you really think I didn't know you've been looking for me all over Paris for weeks? In every hole?" She'd talked herself into such a frenzy that she lost track of what else she wanted to say, and nearly lost her voice, which trailed off while spitting out the last few sentences.

Fec had managed not to interrupt her, possibly to hear the truth, and waited a moment, hoping Bichette would continue.

Yet she didn't because she sensed he was waiting, and also because she wouldn't have been able to speak coherently for much longer. As she walked, she kept tapping the sand with her parasol in time and smiled as if thinking of something very distant.

“Eh OK, I’m sure you knew I was looking for you . . .” At that moment it was more important to Fec that he say something rather than what was said. “It was only natural you’d find out.”

“On the day I arrived in Paris I knew you were just a few hours behind.”

“Did that — surprise you?”

“Yeah. Because I found out about it from you.” Bichette observed him curiously from the side.

“Don’t make silly jokes!” But as soon as he said this, Fec remembered that he . . . He at once saw Pimpi’s pomaded hair sticking up stiffly.

But then Bichette said it: “I was standing behind the door when you were talking to Pimpi from the hall.”

“That’s that.” Fec couldn’t help feeling a twinge of anger. “That’s why he wouldn’t let me in. And that’s why he asked me where you were . . .”

“Pimpi was the first one I went to. I went straight to him from the train station.”

“The doorman was well instructed.” Fec gritted his teeth.

Bichette nodded, moving her tongue back and forth behind her open lips. “You have my compliments though.”

Fec remained standing, legs akimbo, angry because he suspected another humiliation was about to drop.

Bichette smiled obligingly. “My compliments on leaving Menton so quickly. Actually, that’s what impressed me the most of everything you’ve done. How did you manage it? You came by car, eh? You were covered in dust. I could see that through the crack.”

“Yes.” Fec walked on calmly.

"But you only had . . . maybe three hundred francs."

"One hundred and fifty."

"So, an opportunity."

"No. I had wired Laugier for three thousand." Fec, only now remembering he hadn't told Bichette anything about his last meeting with Laugier, recounted it to her, quietly triumphant.

"Why did you keep it from me?" shouted Bichette.

"I forgot."

"Forgot? You don't forget anything!" Bichette didn't try to hide her anger.

"True." Fec blew his nose, especially loudly, just to further annoy Bichette. "For example, later, after Flinsparker wrote the check out to me, I didn't forget to be astonished that he had no idea he'd been fleeced. Because I knew he kept his checkbook in his wallet. Eh OK."

"What do you mean by that, eh?" Bichette didn't even notice how ridiculous her indignation was. "Besides, you lied. You simply played your card."

"Card?" Fec didn't understand right away.

"Isn't it obvious? Laugier isn't that *stupid*."

"Ah . . ." Fec thought hard. "Ha, now I get it! Yes, of course! Yes, *that's* how it was! Like that, and no other way!"

"What're you talking about?"

"From Flinsparker," Fec said, briefly sticking a finger between this teeth. "The first time you came to me that night at the hotel in Monte Carlo, he was gambling in the casino. He won the fifteen thousand and gave it to you shortly before the second time you came to me. That's why you didn't use the vase in the hallway. It occurred to me then, though only for a moment, that you had deviated from this important detail. You also told me about the money without my even asking. And pulled it — out of your stocking." Fec lowered his eyes, so sure was he. "Well, have I guessed it?"

"Partly." His perspicacity and how close he had come to guessing the truth astonished Bichette. And oddly, on this point she didn't lie, despite her penchant for it. "Flinsparker, of course, wanted to show off to me right from the start, and he gave me twenty thousand francs to gamble with and accompanied me to the casino. Since I'm never lucky at gambling, I bet in a way to keep losses low. While Flinsparker was talking to friends, I ran to the hotel, saw the chalk number, and came to you. Then around three in the morning, when he'd lost fifty thousand francs and didn't have another sou in his pocket and was totally blotto, I still had around fifteen of my twenty thousand, with which I . . ." She bit her lower lip, watching Fec, ". . . wanted to make you happy. Once we were in the room, he collapsed into bed like a sack of potatoes and . . ."

Fec stopped and stared at her.

Bichette shuddered. "I will never make sense of you."

Fec struggled to maintain his composure. "So . . . when you came to me the second time around three o'clock . . . you . . . you hadn't even slept with Flinsparker?"

"*That's* it?" Bichette swayed her hips, giggling nastily. "Sssss, slack that is! The guy loses his mind because it didn't happen . . . Oh, I see. You're mad you acted like such a dipshit even though nothing at all happened, eh?"

"Did he at least kiss you?" Fec's face twisted with impatience.

"Why do you care?"

Fec punched his fist in his hand. "*Did* he kiss you or not?"

"He *didn't* kiss me." Bichette, who didn't know how best to annoy Fec, also didn't know how best to lie. "I mean, he kissed me in the car on the drive to Monte and then again at the hotel. A little. Just like an American. But not even a peck later."

"Hmm. Is this the truth?" Fec's eyes burned.

Bichette, who hadn't lied, shrugged and walked on.

Fec followed her, grinning oddly. "When you came to my room at three o'clock in the morning, hours had passed since the last kiss. Yes or no?!"

Bichette turned around and shouted: "What's wrong with you? Have you completely lost it?" She spat at his feet.

Fec stepped up beside her and took her by the arm as they walked. "Eh OK, it's alright."

Bichette tore herself away from him. "*What* do you still want from me?" She gave him a painful poke in the ribs. "Still not cured?"

"The whole story has become rather mysterious." Fec smiled and tightened his scarf.

"You don't believe me."

"No."

"Not even that I just wanted to make you fall in love with me."

"No. You never spit out everything."

Bichette twisted her mouth. "Haven't I made it absolutely clear to you?"

"No. Some of your evidence is contradictory and some of it just motives a posteriori."

"What?" Bichette was angry she didn't understand these words. "You phony phrasing fathead!"

"You're ingenious." Fec's nose twitched. "But I'm not nearly ready to make it so easy for you to lie to me. That's why I will refrain from poking holes in your story with the many small contradictions and will just limit myself to the most glaring . . . Eh OK, how come you thought I was the only man who could run away from you at a time when you already had a man you were chasing? Probably because he ran away from you once before?"

Bichette put her fingers under her chin. "Pimpi."

"Certainly."

"He's just my poodle." But Bichette immediately regretted not having just lied.

"You're naïve."

"Who knows, all my viewpoints might be off base."

Fec felt as if he remembered something. But he couldn't quite get a handle on what because he was too eager to break Bichette's pride. "So, *who* beat you?"

Bichette looked at him in amazement. "Who, me . . . ? Oh, that was Loute."

"Loute? I doubt it."

Bichette again flew into a rage. "What if I told you she'd been looking for me for weeks, just like you and just like Ralix? And that she caught me on the street two days ago? Unfortunately, I was dressed too well. My jacket was too tight, and my skirt. That's why she got the better of me. Otherwise . . . à la Saint-Glinglin. But it was good of her to drag you into Liberty's Bar. Just — a miscalculation."

"A coincidence, in my opinion."

"How sure of himself he is!" Bichette scrutinized him slowly. "It was *no* coincidence. It *was* intentional. She discovered what hotel I was staying at, as she did before, and was keeping an eye on me. She dragged you there because she hoped I would take the offered revenge out on her in your presence no matter what. She was just waiting for me to give her a sign. Then we would've taken it outside, chosen a deserted backstreet, and then . . . Bah! And if I'd gone for it, she probably would've stabbed me in the back. To get her Ralix back. *Her* Ralix! Riche, eh?"

For no particular reason Fec was convinced this explanation was likely accurate, and for that very reason it gave him even greater pleasure to continue to doubt her. "But she even avoided dancing with me. Generally speaking, her behavior was rather cautious."

Bichette looked contemptuously at the ground. "To show me how certain she felt about you."

"Hmm." Fec blew his nose. "Are you also telling me this to make me fall in love with you?"

"You mooncalf!" Bichette's mouth twisted in indescribable disdain while simultaneously returning the lecherous smile of a passerby, who responded with a pitying look at her companion.

Fec saw her grin at this and smiled. "Maybe you just ran away so I would run after you? To *make* me fall in love with you . . . for effect?"

"I know how clever you are with deduction." Bichette slowly licked her upper lip. "But maybe you'd do better to point out a few of those contradictions to me."

"Gladly." Fec approached her again and walked close

beside her. "Eh OK, how is it you really fancied me when I was drunk and made this terrific, this lovely, this delightful deal, even though you didn't like said deal at all? And how is it that you had the exquisite intention to make me fall in love with you and then to leave me, even though you wanted me to leave you to prove my love?"

"Rotter!" Bichette stood in his way, planting her parasol in the sand in front of her. "If you think I . . ."

"I'm not finished yet. And how is it that you *did* everything you did to make me fall in love with you, even though the purpose you claim to be behind is so variable?" Fec propped up a leg and lit a cigarette.

Bichette suddenly lowered her eyes. She had turned red.

Fec knew right away she would never forgive herself for it, so he decided to come to her aid, perhaps not to cut her off from him entirely. "It's something completely different. You're immensely proud. You defend yourself against every man. And are especially fierce against someone you fear might one day dominate you. You defended yourself against me, too. Right from the start. I felt it even on the first night when we walked from the Léon to the Aëro. You said then that every man bored you. You said it only because it was the first time I'd said something delicate . . . Ah, now I know what you were alluding to earlier . . . You thought it best straight off to guard yourself against such subtleties lest I gain the upper hand . . . And I already felt it when you were looking at the yellow wool cap in the mirror on Rue Démours, and then smiling at me as you walked. I couldn't decide at the time in what way. Today I know that it was a smile certain of victory . . . And I was sure of it when you so vehemently said, staring at the streetlamp, that you could no longer be on idle. This stare was directed right at me, and your strange smile shortly after confirmed it. And I almost knew it when you refused to repeat what you had said at Hotel Puget after the altercation with the Japanese guy. Today I know what it was you said then. Not word for word, of course. The gist: 'Why are you still standing there?' That was it, roughly." With a quick twist of his foot he crushed the cigarette that had fallen from his mouth.

Bichette abruptly raised her head.

Fec could tell by the wild expression in her eyes that he was on target. He forgot what he had wanted just a moment ago, and whereas before he'd been hesitant, he now spoke with complete confidence. "Eh OK. This 'Why are you still standing there?' was, of course, partly a result of your fatigue. But mostly it was a result of my triumphs, from Gaby's fit of jealousy, to that ace cretin on Avenue des Ternes, to my knocking out the Japanese guy. The extra advantage I got from this bothered you. You had to defend yourself against it. But since you realized how carelessly you had behaved, you took care not to repeat it. You were also angry with me because of Pimpi. You were worried about him and blamed me for his mishap. That's why you tore yourself away from me on the street on the way to the Aëro. And when you pushed me into the chair the next day, you were angry because you were afraid I might've noticed how you really felt about Pimpi. At the time, though, I thought he was just some low-life. As a distraction you started talking about our deal right afterward. And also, it goes without saying, because it generally suited you. You wanted to trap me with it. I called you insincere then because you weren't serious about this deal, as you've already admitted. But only today do I see everything clearly. You made the scene with the jewelry to show it to me. To lure me, hold me, and so make me easier to subdue. And then when we tussled, you only screamed because you were about to lose. You staggered because you lost a heel. I can still see your eyes trained on me, following me until I put the suitcase key in my pocket. At that moment you believed your goal had been achieved. And when you sent me to sell the bracelet, you smiled triumphantly. Rightly so, in part. Because I believed then that all that crap belonged to you. Today I know only some of it can be yours, or none of it. What woman, especially of your ilk, would lead the life you do if she had a small fortune in a valise? Of course you've been given jewelry, but a woman like you doesn't collect it. She wears it or moves it. You don't wear any of it out of caution. In Nice you wore the sapphire agraffe, but in such a way that it was almost invisible. And only because there was no alternative. So for you I was only useful enough to fence Pimpi's loot. You had a victory when I said I was ready to get out of town. But I agreed to it only because I was drunk and didn't really care. You now believed you were close to total victory over me. This explains your sudden burst of enthusiasm in the taxi on the way to the train station. It was less pure theater than perhaps the suggestive display of a particular state of mind, as it was for me. My drunken speech at the Léon came from a similar state of mind. I bet you said to yourself then: 'He's still going on about love, he still wants love, so he's going to make one last harebrained attempt, so he's a mooncalf.' And I bet you had arranged a rendezvous with Pimpi that morning at the Léon. In any case, he was sure to run into you there at that hour. What he told you that afternoon at Hotel Puget, well, he wanted to tell you that morning . . . Ah, yes, now I remember! 'Stupid people make the world such a pretty place.' That was for my benefit. Because Pimpi was lying then. He hadn't gotten your address from Loute. The only reason the manager of the Aëro gave out our new address was because he knew him. Incidentally, this was when I first saw your leather bag with the jewelry. So that's it."

"Shut your trap!" Having thus far listened motionlessly, Bichette bent the parasol between her hands until it cracked, and she took a few steps. "You have a good memory."

"I would be delighted if I could help yours, which isn't too shabby either." Fec pressed her arm tightly, and when she did not pull it away, said softly: "I fear, dear Bichette, we're both simply beyond help."

Bichette opened her lips, smiling vaguely. "But my crap isn't hot. Somebody fed you that bull."

"When you saw the two bags then . . . You looked terrified, as if something terrible had happened . . . as if someone was after you . . ."

Bichette interrupted him very gently: "Pimpi wanted me to get out of town. Because of Ralix. That's why he brought me my crap. The way I live, I need someone to keep it for me. And with no money . . . That's the only reason I sent you to sell it."

"Ralix was the motive. But the reason was me. You can't live without Paris. You just wanted to stay away until Pimpi sorted things out with Ralix. Presumably he still needs to

— sort things out. And you wanted to use those weeks of forced absence — opportunity creates possibilities — to remake *me*." Fec pressed his fingers one by one into her forearm to lend his words an innocuous veneer.

"No, if it weren't for Ralix I definitely *wouldn't* have gone to Nice," Bichette said very firmly.

"And now you're here, even though he's been out for three weeks. So why did you leave Paris, if not for me?"

Bichette was silent, shrugging her shoulders.

Fec was amazed that she was allowing him to grip her arm. In a way it made him happy. "By the way, at Hotel Puget I noticed how you derisively screwed up your mouth when I snapped my fingers in Pimpi's ear as I went to the window. I just hadn't *seen* it yet then and hadn't *heard* the 'herring' remark yet . . . and that Negro laugh of his haha . . ."

Bichette hummed.

"Did that clever poodle Pimpi at least take the loot back from you? When you were standing behind the door, you must've enjoyed seeing me toss him a hundred francs. Or maybe he actually needed it? I wouldn't put it past *you*."

"Merci." Bichette was still humming. "I was more pleased to see you so animated. Certainly not because of Gaby, eh?"

"No, because of you." Fec squeezed her arm so tightly she almost screamed.

"Or because of . . ." Bichette's fingers made the motion of counting money.

Fec was now in a good mood. "You *didn't* have more than all my other women."

"Nettly, that is."

"Before, when you said the opposite, you wanted to hide

the fact that you had betrayed yourself. Anyway, I understood it differently, because otherwise . . . Did you really spend two years at a finishing school?"

Bichette laughed and blew into his eyes. "I only said that because I . . . In the little hotel near the station in Nice, after we went to the Jetée for the first time, you told me all sorts of things . . . your stories about elegant women, your past exploits, which I believed coming from you, even before that old roly-poly indirectly confirmed it all."

"You still haven't told me why you claimed you spent two years at a finishing school." Fec asked again, although he understood exactly what she had wanted to insinuate.

"Couci-couça, why not?" Bichette still squirmed a bit. "I said it because I was annoyed . . . because I was afraid I wouldn't be able to compete on that point . . . or something. Me — in a finishing school!" It was clear by her tone that she regretted her candor and was now getting aggravated again. "My father was a butcher, but before that he spent seven years in prison. And my mother died at Saint-Lazare, poisoned by a sausage. I think she was . . ." she suddenly laughed hoarsely, ". . . a pompous old bat."

"I didn't know you were so — sensitive."

"Sensitive? I'd like to know who between us is the more sensitive." Bichette whistled. "I'm not much different from you. Do you know what bugged me most?"

Fec thought it over. And since his many recapitulations made it easier for him to peruse the matter, he quickly came up with something. "Ah! When I proposed the Flinsparker scam to you on the promenade in Nice my demeanor was so cold and businesslike . . . The way you caressed your breasts at that moment . . . That's what bothered you the most, wasn't it?"

"Yeah, then. But most of all . . . Do you remember how you said you had 'completely fallen under this spell'? I found *that* incredibly annoying. You have no idea. I believe if you hadn't said *that,* I would then . . ."

"Then you wouldn't have been so motivated later and wouldn't have left."

"How dare you! That's riche!" Bichette freed her arm and walked faster.

"Now you understand what I mean by creating motives a posteriori."

"Bah!" Bichette turned pale because she felt she couldn't bear being wrong any longer.

"Eh OK, then I'll just have to tell you. This whole revelation of your secret to me, this whole making-me-fall-in-love-with-you story, it's just a fabrication your little head has cleverly crafted to crush me. To satisfy your boundless pride. And it needed this satisfaction, because you were actually in love with me for a while. Just remember how you suddenly kissed my sleeve in the little bouillon on Rue Lépic, and how later at Moulin de la Galette you played with my hair during one of the last dances . . . how you always toyed with my cap . . . in your lap."

"Shut your trap!" In a flash Bichette turned to him her trembling face, glowing with hatred. "*Who* cheated you of your share? *Who* stole from you? *Who* dumped you with three . . . with a hundred and fifty francs and an unpaid hotel bill of more than six hundred francs? *Who . . . ?*"

"You, you, you . . . eh OK, you!" Fec grinned in delight.

"For a very plausible reason. Revenge. Since your love remained unrequited, you wanted at least to draw my anger. My anger at such a heavy financial loss. And now your double anger, since you realize that I've seen through you and not only am I not angry about being taken for a ride by you, but on the contrary am . . . how should I put it — delighted by it."

Bichette said in a completely different voice: "You can't possibly believe that I was . . . let's say — in love with you."

Fec was so stunned to hear this hollow little voice that he almost felt ashamed. Yet he quickly clicked his tongue indifferently. "In any case, as you must *now* admit, you were wrong about the money. Very wrong. Of course, you couldn't have known how irrelevant this everyday trifle is to me."

"You're right, *that* I couldn't have known." Bichette laughed disgustingly. "How much do you want? That's the whole point of all this tralala anyway."

". . . it's called an adventure!" exclaimed Fec.

"Huh? . . . Adventure? You're a total kook."

Fec had to sneeze.

Bichette giggled. "He sneezes at it too. He sneezes."

Fec felt at once as if liberated, as if lifted out of himself, as if at a remove from everything he'd allowed to torment him in his extreme fatigue. He sang in a voice clear and light: "J'ai une femme qui aime les animaux, ça c'est rigolo, ça c'est rigolo . . ."

"Ça c'est rigolo . . ." Bichette kicked him.

"You only love animals. And rightly so."

"Shnuk!"

"And the Japanese guy? And Pimpi? And Ralix?"

"Pimpi? . . . No."

"A yellow ape, a poodle, and a zebra."

"Jokes!" Bichette seemed to be struggling with herself. And suddenly she spat it out, scathingly: "Pimpi's my brother."

It mattered so little to Fec whether he should believe her or not that he pretended to believe her. "So that's why he got to visit you so often. Shortly before we left for Nice, when I came back to the hotel with your skirts and shoes, he had stopped by again."

"Did you run into him?"

"No. There was the smell of him, though barely perceptible, so I thought I might be mistaken. Even when we were still staying at the Aëro, he must've come by to see you often."

"Yeah. Did you know?"

"No. But when you had that sobbing fit and ran out of the room, it did flash through my mind: 'She only did that to meet someone outside.' It was only for a second, though. I immediately forgot about it. Now, of course . . ."

"Listen, Fec," Bichette began after a moment, stammering, "I'll now tell you honestly what the sobbing was all about . . . Yeah, I faked it. Cross that you didn't think I was beautiful."

"Let's drop it, Bichon." Fec was now truly convinced he couldn't believe a word she said, and looked for a way to end the conversation that would be to his benefit. This is why he failed to see Bichette biting her lower lip in agitation.

"Listen, Fec, the first time we slept together in the Aëro, I asked if you thought I was beautiful. You said very coolly — yes. And at Hotel Puget, when I asked you the second time, you said it almost reluctantly. But on the way to the Jetée, you told me I was beautiful. You also said it the day Flinsparker kidnapped me. Both times you said it just to get me in the mood. You didn't want to say that before. It was either to keep me from feeling sexy, or maybe because you actually didn't find me beautiful. Whatever the case, it's how you kept me docile. I really doubted if you found me beautiful, and was so flattered in the taxi I didn't realize what an incredible insult it was not to be told what you were actually up to. I was so pissed off that I followed you so easily. You simply duped me that first night in Nice. You must have had a good laugh at my expense. That's when I started to hate you. And do you know when it came to me that you were just making fun of me? When you told me about your adventures that night in the little hotel near the train station. Then I realized how spoiled you'd been and was afraid I wasn't pretty enough for you. That's why I was so unbearable the next day on the balcony at Hotel Ruhl. Bing, now you know."

"If that's really the way it was," said Fec carelessly, "then you should've been upset *about that*. Not just about the whole spell thing. Why has all this occurred to you so late? You're just looking for justifications. That's all."

Bichette was about to start up again but stopped herself just in time. "You can't control memory. But I suppose it's no less understandable. I wanted to test the extent of my power . . . because a woman, after all, has no other . . . and I was livid that your only response was yes."

Oddly enough, Fec couldn't fathom the depth of Bichette's humiliation, but he at least could sense that the moment had come for her to make her retreat. Still, he was held back by an acute, subtle mistrust that he was at a loss to explain. "Let's drop it."

"Yeah, let's drop it," Bichette repeated with slightly feigned bravado. "Let's drop it . . ." After a while she opened her handbag and rummaged through the tins, pens, and boxes.

Fec just happened to look and saw her knife. "Ah! . . . Where did you . . . How did you . . ." In one fell swoop his mistrust was given clarity.

"Huh?" Bichette powdered herself briskly.

"Your knife. When I carried you from the Jetée to the hotel, you had it in your hand. That is, I took it from you before. When did you take it back from me? That's twice you've taken it back from me." Fec wondered how he could have forgotten about it so completely. The last thing fell into place in his head.

"Let's drop it." Bichette firmly closed the handbag.

"And — the suitcase key."

"How fragrantly he says that!"

"The end is always a kind of sweet air, my esteemed master."

"And he quotes me to boot."

"Actually, I'm quoting myself — through you."

"Versifying again, are you, mooncalf?"

"Idiot!"

"Merci."

They both laughed. It sounded heartfelt without being so. Then they took each other's hands. Neither knew who had taken whose hand first.

"Eh OK, so you are now determined to play the grande demimondaine, so to speak."

"I am . . . in a manner of speaking."

"Well since you're almost even more elegant than you were in Nice, so . . ."

"Nettly. I only did this to spite you."

"Could be. Just not very likely. Like everyone else, you've developed a taste for . . . let's say — the high life. Completely even. And just as quickly."

"Just yak, all of it."

"Nettly, yak . . ." Fec stretched his face upward. Seemingly without realizing it, he let go of Bichette's hand. "It is certainly striking . . . Now, all of a sudden, you remind me of a woman I lived with for months in Rome. Many years ago. It ended very unusually. For days she would lie on the carpet, smoking, eating, and sleeping without undressing. And when I came home at night, I often wasn't even able to hold a conversation. But in the final few weeks it was these conversations that enticed her even more than the way of life she got to experience thanks to me. It seemed to her more and more as if the real reason we were leading this life was only for the sake of these sweet, crazy conversations, as she called them. She ultimately reached a state in which everything, be it a wild life or wild talk, affected her like a narcotic, and she craved stronger and stronger doses. Since the life of adventure no longer had a narcotic effect on her, nor did the greatest excesses of love, nor even the sweet and crazy conversations, which had become, more often than not, repetitive, she felt ever more keenly that everything was coming to an end. Everything seemed already lived, worn out, finished. And it was then, in a state of dull expectation of ever newer intensifications, that she condemned herself to prostration and confinement to the house. She saw nothing ahead of her except the virtual certainty of magnificent success, a great deal of money, maybe millions, which she basically wouldn't know what to do with. And she felt quite clearly that I, too, wouldn't know what to do with such wealth, that all the intense activity that had occupied me for weeks and profoundly bored me only served to keep me distracted. Perhaps it was the state she found herself in, forced to observe everything at a remove, passively. And she remembered certain conversations over and over that ended with a semi-veiled gaze into the gray, the void, into the menacing distance, where she, and I, had fled as if from ourselves, so as not to have to flee from each other, and perhaps even from — everything. *From everything.* There were moments when the impossible, the bitter, the burning, the intolerable nature of her own person, of my own person, of our life together, of the *whole,* penetrated so acutely and deeply into her consciousness that she got up from the carpet, limp and pale, and would have been happy for something totally stupid, totally senseless to happen. She found herself hoping, begging, imploring a vague unknown, a drunken fate, the bearer of something unfathomably stupid, something infinitely stupid and crazy, that would be her salvation." Having spoken more passionately than ever before, Fec's face briefly flashed with impatient anticipation of the story's effect.

But Bichette, already breathless, asked: "And how did it end? What happened then?"

"I became increasingly silent and obstinate with each passing day. Because I recognized very clearly Marcelle's inner catastrophe. I would have . . ."

"Marcelle . . ." whispered Bichette.

Fec seemed not to hear or see anything. "Eh OK, I should've been able to find the right words to express my state of mind and to create a new level, ratcheting up the tension. But then the fantastically voluptuous idea came to me that this time I should do nothing, just push *it all* to the edge, curtail the *final* conversation about the consummation of my genius scheme, which was to bring us the magnificent success and millions, and thereby give her and myself an unprecedented experience, such pleasure, such perplexity, such happiness finely ground . . . unknown . . . bewildering . . . that was to meld us together forever into an ineffable, perhaps unsurpassable, oneness . . . Some moments at night I thought I would pass out from the anticipation, the tension, the pain even. I almost couldn't take it anymore. I . . . shut it, I'm babbling nonsense. I am indeed . . ."

"Oh, you're cute, you're a beaut . . ." Bichette dug her fingers into Fec's shoulder. Her eyes watered. "Henri, you are . . ."

"Henri . . . did you say?" Fec pushed her hand off. It was as if he didn't know what he was doing. "Just like at Moulin de la Galette . . ."

"Oh, you're right . . . you're right . . ." Bichette choked back tears. "But tell me what happened to her, how it was, how it was . . . with Marcelle . . ."

"You know her name?"

"You just said it . . . So go on, talk!"

Fec smiled sympathetically. "Eh OK. It went the way it went. The ending was not routine. That is . . ." he laughed hoarsely, ". . . very routine. The scam was blown. Purely by chance. Because of a — cake shipment, which I took delivery of by mistake. One of those mistakes that would be better called a villainous act of Providence. But with that, everything else also collapsed. All the inner tension I'd carefully nurtured evaporated in a matter of minutes. It ended as it usually does. Unusually ordinary. When the money ran out and there were no prospects in sight, she ditched me for the owner of a racing stable. That's that."

Bichette remained silent for a long time. Her arms trembled. Her feet wriggled. At last, she asked, timorously, curiously: "I don't know . . . Why did I remind you of that woman?"

Fec pretended to be embarrassed. "Why? Because it was probably the same between us . . . Yes, she often said — 'cognac,' like you do — 'nettly' . . . Ah, I don't know . . ."

Bichette's whole body began to shudder. "Fec . . . Fec . . ."

Fec looked her straight in the eye and said coldly, "Haven't you had enough? I think it's high time to be sensible. To stop deluding yourself. To stop letting moods and excesses that have crept in fool you. Then later, with cool head, to feel ashamed and convince yourself it was actually you who *created* them."

"No. Not really." Bichette protested, still very flatly, and immediately became so irked she blushed.

Fec smiled wistfully. "You really can convince yourself of *anything*."

"Haven't you also convinced yourself . . ." Bichette straightened up with effort, ". . . that these moods and excesses, as you say, crept in? Why crept in? They just happen. Pop up unexpectedly. So it all depends on them. On them alone. On nothing else." Since Fec was silent, she added quietly: “And that we throw our pride out the window and just brood over them . . .” And since Fec remained silent, she hissed: “But maybe . . .”

“Ah! A brief silence is all that’s needed to prick your pride and you’re already doubting what you’ve just said. Isn’t that enough for you?”

Bichette groaned: “Oh, you’re horrible! . . . just horrible you are!”

“Maybe,” sneered Fec, “it’s why I want to tell you why I was so insistent about what really happened between you and Flinsparker at the hotel in Monte Carlo. Because, devil knows, I was firmly convinced you had slept with him, and delighted by it because knowing this plunged me into a curious state of excitation . . . Ah, that was . . . When you came to me for the second time that night, you thought I was reluctant to have sex with you because you had already been with Flinsparker . . . On the contrary, my reluctance was because I was so aroused *by it* . . . so much that I bit you . . . Well, I want to let you know now why I bit you . . . That is to say, I didn’t know at the time why I bit you . . . And actually, I don’t know now, either . . .” His eyes suddenly narrowed intently.

“What long eyelashes you have,” Bichette said, as if from sleep. “This is the first time I’ve really noticed them.”

“Ah, now I know . . . I know, I know . . .” Fec cried hoarsely. “It was — rage. Rage that I felt none. Perhaps the ultimate pleasure . . . but so superfluous . . . Nonsense, Bichette, I’m just versifying, versifying . . .” He vigorously tugged at his cap. “Eh OK. And now I had to find out (and I know you weren’t lying) if *nothing* had happened. So this unconfessed desire was enough for excess to overtake me. I talked myself into it. After all, there is no real difference between being swayed by a suggestive mood, an excess, or talking yourself into one. Because you should never allow yourself to be carried away if the actual preconditions for such a mood, for such an excess, are absent. You get sucked in either way . . . And now I want to tell you that what I said earlier about my experience with Marcelle was an invention, spur of the moment, though not all of it. In part to indirectly convey to you the rest of the truth about our relationship, in part to see what effect it would have on you. Eh OK, it worked splendidly. It suggestively put you in a mood. Because my ecstasy, my sweet, beautiful words, were all an act. So I could allow myself the immense pleasure of the finale: you let yourself succumb to that last excess of love because I created the atmosphere for it. *Created.* When the conditions are created, then the excess is also created. We really did *everything* to make each other. Each of us created the moods and excesses of the other. We *created us.*"

"You're lying! Rotter!" Bichette spat right in his face. "Now it's *you* coming up with motives a posteriori!"

"Splendid!" Fec slowly wiped the saliva from his face. "But you're wrong."

"*You're* wrong! After I came to you the first time that night in Monte . . . when you sent me away so quickly, without holding me back, without trying to stop me from fucking Flinsparker . . . I was so angry with you and also to grease up that nitwit of an American, naturally I did it . . . did it with the room waiter in his cubby at the end of the hallway . . . That's right, I sure as hell did! So you see, *you're* the one who's wrong . . ."

“Now it’s *you* with motives a posteriori!”

Bichette bared her teeth and shook both fists under her chin. She screamed: “Oh, you, you . . .”

Fec picked up her parasol and made a quick motion with it. “Now enough of this! For good! Besides, now that everything’s become so wonderfully jumbled it would be quite impossible to ever unravel it and reduce it to exquisitely immaculate nothingness.”

“Filthy nothingness!” Bichette clutched his arm.

“Splendid! Filthy nothingness!”

“Hold on!” groaned Bichette, digging her nails even deeper into his arm. “Hold on!”

Fec pulled Bichette’s hands away, not because of the intense pain but because of his superior bearing. “And lately you really did everything you could to experience something new. ‘What won’t we do? We’d *do* anything.’ That’s what you said at the very beginning of this stimulating conversation. You seem to have forgotten that you shared my opinion earlier when I expressed it and justified haha . . . ‘But in the end it’s *also* nada. Like everything else.’ And *that* you said *even* earlier. Back when you were staring at the streetlamp . . . Ah, what a lovely way to pass the time! In the end, it’s *always* at the root of everything. Just hasn’t helped me much. Nothing and no one can help me anymore. And probably not you either. And so . . .”

“Basta!” Bichette adjusted her shawl, raising her eyebrows as if she were bone-tired.

“Basta!” Fec offered her his hand, which she did not take, and whispered, also because it just occurred to his still-functioning brain: “By the way, I still don’t understand how

I could've missed so many things. For example, when you suddenly said 'rotter!' to yourself when urinating one morning in Hotel Ruhl. And it was after that frenzy of sex! And how when we were having that talk outside Cannes and I corrected your formulation, you replied: 'Then it was a mistake!' And how at the end of that conversation when you said to me, 'You need this picked-up stuff for your own well-being,' you hesitated in alarm. Alarmed that you let something like *that* slip out after we agreed on *this*. You had already renounced renunciation then. Was the delight really so great?"

"It was . . . like everything else."

"The Tigress"

"I suppose I only left just to be on the safe side. So as not to end up being duped by you. I well knew that if you tease people a little at first they become stupid later and when stuffed full you can corner them, then you've got them, because they've got nothing else behind them . . . That's more or less the recipe."

"Ah."

Bichette snatched her parasol from him and grabbed the railing of the Anvers metro station. "Bing. I leave from here." She turned her back to Fec.

"Bichette!"

She had already descended a few steps. Still, she stopped immediately and turned around quickly. "What else do you want?"

"Nothing."

Bichette continued on.

"Nothing!" Fec called after her.

Bichette stopped again. Her mouth gaped open, twisted, and then she started to laugh, "Or do you want . . ." She rubbed her fingers together as if counting money. "So tell me, how much do you want? . . . Louche, that is! . . . Come here!" She opened her little handbag. "Come on, come here!"

Fec, now annoyed she had guessed what he wanted, reluctantly approached.

"How much?"

"Five thousand. A guy's got to live, for shit's sake."

"No more?"

"The fifteen thousand are rightfully yours. You made it look like it was stolen . . . You wanted to avoid being suspected of not having dared to steal it. And you wanted to make a fool of me . . . So my cut is actually only half the amount of the check . . ."

"Shnuk!"

"Eh OK."

Bichette laughed wickedly. "Renunciation is the most sublime pleasure, eh?"

"Shut it, and fork it over already!"

At that exact moment a shot rang out.

XIII

Suffering a fatal head wound, Fec was taken to Lariboisière Hospital.

Bichette, who had been the target, was sitting at his bedside, sobbing uncontrollably.

Ralix had the misfortune of tripping over a little girl and falling. He was arrested immediately. And it was by Tall Georges, the cop, who as usual had been standing on the corner of Rue Blanche and tailed Bichette and Fec, whether as a precaution or by request.

Hearing from Nurse Madelon who had been admitted, Gaby cried her eyes out and managed to persuade the nurse to secretly take her to the mortally wounded man after midnight.

When Nurse Madelon, long regretting her rashness, appeared in the doorway with Gaby in her arms, Fec died without regaining consciousness for even a few seconds.

Pimpi closed his eyes, which had been fixed on the ceiling and hideously rolled back in his head.

After his eyes were shut, Bichette, standing pale and tearless at the foot of the bed, said: "His face has every expression."

Pimpi was about to nod in agreement but right then noticed Nurse Madelon. His astonished head froze in an odd position. At last he recognized Gaby, who was staring at Fec's face with an expression of unspeakable anxiety.

Seeing that Fec was dead, she began to curse Bichette with truly impressive viciousness.

Nurse Madelon yelled at Pimpi to shove a handkerchief into Gaby's mouth. He had to do it, whether he wanted to or not . . .

As Bichette followed Pimpi down the wide stairs of the hospital, she said quietly to herself: "Did I love him? Did he love me? Oh God, if only I knew! I think I'm losing my mind."

•

She didn't lose her mind, but she did gain fame. All the newspapers were talking about her. *Le Matin* even ran her picture on the front page and a long article titled "Bichette — la Tigresse," which presented her biography, embellished in typical tabloid fashion; and *Le Journal* devoted an entire feature section to her under the sensational headline: "Mistress of the Murdered Con Man Henri Rilcer." Other tabloids compared her to La Goulue, the great coquette of the Moulin Rouge, or to Grille d'Egout, even though she bore no resemblance whatsoever, or accurately referred to her as the "Jane Avril of the gutter."

In short, Bichette had become a celebrity overnight and, less proud but more scornful than ever, she jumped on — quite literally — the offer made in haste by a grain magnate from southern Russia. She became his mistress, and after three weeks bashed his head in with an iron umbrella stand, then managed to abscond with Pimpi's help.

•

After the initial excitement over this new bloody event had subsided in the cafés of Montmartre, the debates over the facts began. Audacious theories buzzed around the tables: Fec and Henri Rilcer were in fact not the same person; Bichette had been hired by Armenian rivals; Pimpi had engineered the whole thing and was a spy in the pay of the Japanese, etc., etc. But no consensus was reached this time, either. Unanimity existed on only a single point: that Fec had been an arrant fool after all.

Written in 1921

I . . .

. . . was born on March 15, 1889, in Karlsbad. The town is where I attended gymnasium and where I first encountered a subtle mind, in the form of Roman writer Publius Ovidius Naso, and human depravity, in the form of the teaching staff. I was considered to be a subversive element, although at that time I was only interested in chambermaids and did my earnest best to honor the aforementioned writer. I never completed my studies of law, which I began at the age of eighteen. I studied Vienna instead, a very commendable city then. It is still a mystery to me today how I passed the state examination in legal history. Shortly thereafter, I had a stroke of luck at a Munich carnival, and with my last gold coin from the winnings went to Berlin, where I was bored for two weeks because I slept at night. When I began to do things the other way around, I so thoroughly enjoyed myself for three years that my love for this city remains as ineradicable as my love for its argot. Since someone had kept me enrolled in Vienna behind my back, I could not resist the temptation to see my debts paid insofar as I planned to spend four months dozing through courses in Greifswald. The result was nevertheless positive, for which I have Ovid to thank. I worked him into the oral exam, and since my examiners were connoisseurs of human nature and true humanists, I earned a *juris utriusque doctor*. It served me well for a long time. For I soon decided not to pursue the prescribed career (is there not a more beautiful phrase?), but to travel around Europe. The patriarch of a family who notices someone not leading a bourgeois way of life is, generally speaking, immediately convinced he is leading a criminal one. Only an unbridled imagination could reveal to him the vast field of possibilities that lie between these two poles. A doctorate, however, delays that conviction by stimulating the imagination in a civic-minded way. Be that as it may, when the Great War broke out, I was already held in such disrepute that my four-year forced sojourn in Switzerland afforded me a variety of distractions and, moreover, with the leisure to write a Handbook for all, titled *Last Loosening,* whose ultimate point is that one's determination is of far more value than experience. In the Alps, for which I have not the slightest affection, I also wrote the 33 outlandish stories that make up the collection *At the Blue Monkey,* which, for all its high praise by some discerning minds, cemented my deplorable reputation. When the war ended, I got back on the train. I must confess that I am already bored with it. But of all the pleasant things the world isn't particularly rich in, it is the least enervating. The only thing I find genuinely perturbing is that the most loathsome conduct is continually attributed to me. I therefore solemnly declare: that I am neither a brothel owner nor the right-hand man of Boris Savinkov, whom I unfortunately did not know personally; that I love the Berlin-N-Junge, but consider the German double mocha a nasty swill; that I consider dealing with people to be psycho-dancing and Lichtenberg's aphorisms and Flaubert's *November* good for preschool; that I miss the

Austrian Memphis cigarette, but not the lieutenants who would consume them en masse; that I use my much loved Jicky perfume by means of an atomizer and fail to understand those who because of this deny me any capacity for intelligence; that politics makes me retch, but I am fond of the Italian lazzo; that I am sensitive, lazy, curious, and crass; that I consider many French women to be exquisite creatures, but most Russians to be hysterics; that I travel neither at the behest of Škoda nor of the Emperor of the Sahara, but for my own pleasure; and that I have a Czechoslovak passport and, fortunately, thick skin.

Walter Serner

Die neue Bücherschau, Berlin, June 1925
Karlsbader Tagblatt, no. 143, Karlsbad, June 26, 1925
Radikaler Geist, Berlin, 1930

The Maupassant of Crime Fiction
by Theodor Lessing

Czechoslovakia is fertile ground for the imagination. Its soil is a strange mixture. A fruitful tension fills its air. Young Slavs striving for the intellectual spirit, the miraculous power of the ancient German tongue, Jewish spirituality turning back to its motherland . . . it is a fact: the brilliant masters and critics of the word are concentrated in and around the Prague of today. But neither Rilke's somewhat pampered verbal unity, nor Werfel's wild linguistic beauty, nor Brod's fiercely sober logic, nor Mauthner's overly clever critique of language, nor Kafka's classically pure discipline, nor Kisch's always objective bulls-eye, nor Kuhscher's verbal frenzy, nor Wiener, Salus, Adler, not one of these has resonated so much with me as the gruesome style of the most dubious of all the profound minds of Bohemia, so cold and insolent is it that in comparison Sternheim merely spouts sentimentalities, and he is certainly a "man of letters." This man's name is Walter Serner. He is a psychologist's dream, but let the reader be forewarned.

I cannot say much about the man himself. In order to obtain some clues, I contacted his publisher. His reply, which I was given express permission to use, is as follows:

"Mr. Serner, in whom you are so interested, is 35 years old and hails from Teplitz. His father is a German Jew, his mother a Czech. He ended up at an early age on the so-called slippery slope and has roamed the globe his entire life. You will not find his address in literary almanacs, but you can certainly get it from the criminal justice authorities. He is a world-class international con man. He spent his apprenticeship in Paris as a costel (pimp). Nowhere in his books will you find anything he himself has not experienced. You are free to share all this, Mr. Serner doesn't give a damn. He is currently traveling the Orient as the proprietor of large brothels in Argentina."

So says the publisher, Mr. Stegemann [sic]. How refreshing that one is able to plainly praise here a principled absence of principles that would otherwise be met with libel charges in civic life.

Oscar Wilde once wrote about Thomas Griffiths Wainewright: "The fact of a man being a poisoner is nothing against his prose." Thus Mr. Serner's trade should not prejudice nor alter the fact that this contemporary author is of a stature equal to Rubens and Shakespeare: a Rubens of all trials and tribulations, a Shakespeare of dreadful lusts and vices. He has written the following five books: *The Eleventh Finger*, *At the Blue Monkey*, *The Whistle Around the Corner*, *The Tigress*, and *Last Loosening*. Three of them were published by Paul Stegemann [sic!], the others by Elena Gottschalk Verlag. They include short stories featuring crooks, snitches, strumpets, and swindlers, stories in the tradition of Maupassant. *The Tigress* is a short novel; *Last Loosening* is an introduction to the "philosophy of Dada," a book that is nothing more than a joke, and not a very good one at that. For a joke to be good, some kind of meaning has to be lurking behind it. Incidentally, smashing a hundred streetlamps is no wittier than smashing one. Of all of Serner's books, I rank *The Tigress* at the top, a great achievement bereft of creative force and art, but as obsessed with life as a writhing ball of worms and scorpions stinging each other. In order to convey an idea of this tremendous novel, in which a feverish air circulates without anything happening, I will have to try to decant the cider from the bottle of the "problem."

The eponymous Tigress is a redheaded, piercingly beautiful, panther-like, wild cocotte of Montmartre, carefree and proud, loving nothing but the perpetual stupefaction of her boundless boredom and the satisfaction of her unpredictable appetites. Her equally stalwart partner (a self-portrait of the author) is a grifter, globetrotter, and gambler in life on a grand scale, contemptuous of all. These two fish-cold, completely vacuous souls are only receptive to the most outrageous tricks of the nerves and mental frenzies. Feeling each other out, the two perfidious, unloving yet sovereign natures make a resolution: to love each other and elevate each other to all-dominating Übermenschen. Similar to the hero in Paul Bourget's *Le Disciple*, they begin in cold cynicism, one outdoing the other, to then experiment with themselves and with each other. They subject their feelings to "picked-up stuff," while observing and analyzing each other in the process. It soon becomes impossible to distinguish where the truth of this affective life ends and where it begins as an act. Whenever a sliver of nature slips through, it is immediately exploited, interpreted, and deflated by these ice-cold underworld operators. Oftentimes their excesses are just chilly hypocrisy, but genuine excesses still exert unconscious pressure on them; at other times, something definitive bursts forth from a kind of cocaine-fueled paralysis of the soul. The pursuit of ever greater thrills and tensions in life leads to a madness that is a true reflection of civilized humanity.

We are faced with having to traverse impenetrably real emotional floods and surges of fabricated and feigned sensations. Suppose we assume that Serner is simply "annoyed," and does not know whether his rage is affected or genuine; for if a bit of nature should ever penetrate this most conscious of all conscious self-observers, his prideful con-man superiority will immediately detect and utilize it, observing the highest commandment: "Stay sharp." This intersection of every *primitive* stimulation and debauchery with *intentional* states of mind meshes into a delicious mockery of all the doctrinal nonsense grown-up children blather about "psychoanalysis"; so much is always overlooked, before, after, and in the midst. The only end for Serner's hyperconscious, clairvoyant doppelgänger is madness, but the author prefers to cut the thread with a senseless death. The Tigress returns to her milieu, the demimonde, and doesn't even know herself if she has now loved, or only made love? The reader is also at a loss to determine whether these two people were merely deluding themselves all along, or if they truly experienced each other. A psychologist would likewise be at a loss.

Serner has also written about a hundred short stories. They exhibit a lack of everything that makes a poet: musicality, a sense of nature, landscape, mood, silence, humor. But in their unsurpassable cold and clever impudence they are so brimming with the human condition and life that even Satan himself with his icy hand could not write it any better. To fully appreciate this brilliance, I recommend the story "Sprat

Smooches" from the collection *The Whistle Around the Corner*. I confidently make this assertion: no living writer can match this truth. Ultimately, it's an unnaturalness resembling Sternheim's buffooneries, born of a desire to render speaking figures constantly visible, turned agonizing. Serner registers movements, yet since he is neither a seer nor a dreamer, but a cerebral man, all the rummaging, cramping, scratching, licking, and tugging never become vivid for the imagination. Yet wherever this devilish fellow turns his mind, a perspicacity emerges from which every psychologist has a thing or two to learn . . . And now I do not quite know why I have even written this. One might rightly ask: Why should I enter this hell? After all, we are to avoid Satan's realm. Well, yes, and no. The thing is: However many crimes and sins one is able to endure without suffering harm is no measure of one's worth, but is a measure of one's strength. Imagine a Kant or a Schiller transported to this world, even for a single month — they would surely perish, utterly. Although how inconsiderate to do something like this, to drop someone into the thick of things and extract truths that neither a Schiller would ever see nor a Kant ever comprehend. Yet madness and crime are also life. And even the inhuman is human. Although one may (rightly) reject all this, Goethe's words remain apt:

> Persuaded I can never be,
> Don't belittle the devil to me:
> There must be something in a man
> So hated by all mankind!

Prager Tagblatt, no. 109, Prague, May 10, 1925

*Theodor Lessing and the Sex Trafficker**
by Walter Serner

When Theodor Lessing's article on me, "The Maupassant of Crime Fiction," appeared in the *Prager Tagblatt* in May of last year, I did not refute the information he repeated in it that had been supplied by my former publisher Paul Steegemann, who claimed I was "a pimp, world-class international con man, and proprietor of large brothels in Argentina." (My short autobiography, published soon after in *Die neue Bücherschau*, was already in the publisher's possession for many months and at his disposal on this occasion.)

It is not my custom to debunk personal attacks against me. If I now choose to do so with regards to the statements made by Mr. Steegemann, it is not done to redress my civic honor. Today, hundreds of people who rightly belong in prison enjoy their civil rights, especially in the larger countries. So to me, who will refrain here from any personal

* This is Serner's response not to Lessing's article of the previous year per se, but to the vicious attacks directed at him for writing it. Filled with anti-Semitic bile, the vilifications that appeared in print even included the notorious Nazi ideologue Alfred Rosenberg, whose text in *Der Weltkampf* of July 1925, titled "International Sex Trafficking," ended with the line: "For the Jew life means creating mold and then acting as a worm in it."

opinion, this ambition could hardly matter. What has prompted me to publicly denounce these claims has been the shameful smears of an irreproachable man who can be accused of nothing more than having had the courage to speak the truth, even though he is not independent.

Mr. Steegemann claimed there is nothing in my books that I have not personally experienced. This is true. Things I have seen or heard, and often even things I have experienced firsthand, lie behind every line I have written. But to identify my life with the realities portrayed in my fiction is by no means the irrefutable fact many might assume. It would be difficult to find an author who is more conversant with Europe's criminal underworld and who has described it more honestly than have I, but is it really so implausible that someone might move within this milieu without actually participating in its activities? It would seem so. Even the police detectives who've had me under surveillance for six years in every country of Europe have shown they do not believe it plausible either: anyone such as I, so familiar with criminals and the work of the police, either must be a criminal himself or an enemy secret agent. That someone might acquire such knowledge merely through observation seems inconceivable to any criminologist. And yet it is so. The fact that I have an absolutely spotless criminal record and there is no actual evidence of any wrongdoing by me would only serve as proof of my criminal genius. While this is indeed flattering, it is not true.

The truth is that I have never been a pimp, never an international con man, never a sex trafficker. It would be easy for me to prove what I have lived on up to now. And it is a joke of tragicomic proportions that the few indiscretions in my life have been caused by the constraints the police have seen fit to impose on me. These days, such indiscretions are no barrier to someone serving as a government minister. Yet there is no one who could produce conclusive and credible evidence to the contrary to what I have stated.

Admittedly, my refutation fails to touch on the essentials of the savage attacks against Theodor Lessing, but rather on the inessential; yet this, unfortunately, is precisely the essential point here. For Theodor Lessing has lavished praise on my literary work with the utmost superlatives without knowing me personally and without approving of the life my work depicts or my private life, which he has assumed to be one and the same. He praised my work as he would praise Shakespeare's tragedies without identifying with the moral code of the murderers therein. Had Shakespeare been a murderer, his dramas would be none the worse, and neither would Theodor Lessing's appraisal. From the standpoint of bourgeois morality, Lessing has merely done in the current case what every one of his professional colleagues has so often done, at least verbally, in the antiquated case of Shakespeare: he has approved of a work that depicts immorality in the bourgeois sense as being sincere and well-written. And lo and behold, a mob suddenly rears its head and hurls scorn and contempt in his face, because the author of the work he has praised is de facto a sex trafficker. Who sees the difference? The most inessential has been turned into the most essential.

So, by calling the inessential untrue and denying the possibility of rebuttal, the screamers in effect undermine their essential argument. They may limit themselves to the inessential and salute the black-white-red flag: the "half-Jew" Theodor Lessing, an opponent of imperialism, has aroused their hatred, nothing more.

Karlsbader Tagblatt, no. 149, Karlsbad, July 4, 1926

Expert Opinion from Alfred Döblin

NOVEMBER 23, 1931

Expert opinion on the petition to place the book The Tigress *by Walter Serner, published by Paul Steegemann, Berlin, on the "List of Trash and Smut Writings."*

The State Youth Welfare Office of the Rhine Province has submitted a petition, a copy of which the publisher has provided me. The reason for bringing this case to my attention is undoubtedly my position on Serner's work, of which the publisher is aware and which I have also publicly expressed on several occasions, e.g., in *Die neue Rundschau.*

The justification for the petition likely represents the most egregious effort made in this area. I well understand that the Youth Welfare Office of the Rhine Province includes men and women of different confessions and from different cultural spheres of German intellectual life. And the fact that Serner, for example, is being ostracized on the basis of ideological aversion is also understandable. But the fact that this ideological aversion (and such a rationale is thus far legally prohibited, as expressly stated in the "anti-trash and -smut law"), that this ideological-cultural-political aversion should disguise itself in this way, dressing itself up in such a presumptuous form — that is something I have never experienced before as someone who has regularly served in an expert capacity for many such cases and as a member of the Senate of the Prussian Academy of Arts, Dept. of Poetry. The justification made by the Youth Welfare Office of the Rhine Province is enough to make the blood boil of anyone with an honest interest in literature. I shall explain the reasons for my opinion.

The Y.W.O.'s "justification" begins: "This story is utter nonsense." To refute this, I will briefly recount the gist of the story. It is the — not actually and never-ending — struggle of two human natures — situated outside the bourgeois world and its morals — with each other and with their particular environment. The story depicts these amoral creatures of nature — and how! dazzlingly, in the most authentic and crystal-clear hues, as if painted by someone who creates his own colors — how they find each other, in that milieu — how they then, in their own way, parasitically attack their environment, while their terrible, tiger-like love struggle continues unabated — as in the animalistic, natural-historical sphere, into which hardly a ray of bourgeois ethics falls — how they tear themselves apart and cannot separate (for at heart not only is she a tigress, but she holds onto him because she recognizes the tiger in him) — and how the end of this struggle and the story cannot be any other than as told: he perishes among criminals, randomly, almost by chance, as loaded revolvers are always lying around — and she rages on and will come to an end much like Zola's Nana and others.

According to the Y.W.O. of the Rhine Province, this is "utter nonsense." In fact, it is a powerful theme that we will never cease to tackle. And the theme has been adapted by

Serner, severely, seriously, harshly, without concession to any shocked sense of decorum, nor even without resorting to cheap confrontation with a bourgeois person or group in the realm of morality. Nature and amorality are intrinsic to themselves. I need not state here that it would be impossible for an artist, just as with a philosopher and natural scientist, to refer to amorality as immorality. Serner is not doing that. The moralists can write their own stories. Did not Voltaire, Stendhal, and Nietzsche make the distinction clear, illustrating the amorality of nature, which is far from being the same as immorality? And do they not know this in the Rhineland? It comes down to the basic approach. Serner is a naturalist and an amoralist. Whoever attacks him should not resort to such transparent subterfuges. What an imposition it is for him to "find a word of disapproval and disgust for these goings-on," because reading it would imperil the youth. *He has his basic approach! It all depends on his basic approach.* Serner's basic approach (he is a physician) is that of the naturalist and amoralist. His amorality, represented by the men I have mentioned, is as well founded as any other worldview. It is notoriously at war with others. This petition is also a bellicose gesture. And according to the law, the forum of the Review Board is not the place where this battle should be fought.

So much for the general content and robustly authentic basic approach. It is characteristic of the petitioner that they have not even recognized this basic approach and see here, or so it seems, "pornography." Indeed, perhaps Nietzsche was just a "heretic"? and Sigmund Freud simply "immoral"?

The judgments about the work are, in fact, shockingly

clueless, exhibiting the most bloody-minded dilettantism. To draw attention to its dangers, I have also informed our Senate of this "justification." It is simply asserted, merely stated, that the criminal milieu is poorly portrayed. One would have to ask: where and when has the author of the justification acquired knowledge of the criminal demimonde of Paris. Until proven otherwise, this disparaging remark will have to be regarded as nothing more than gratuitous and irrelevant. I, for one, with my knowledge of the Berlin criminal underworld, was delighted by the details and the characterizations — it is not much different over there than it is here.

"The author resorts to a filthy jargon, that is, for one with an abiding appreciation for the German language, downright embarrassing." I myself have read such sentiments in newspapers and magazines about my last book, *Berlin Alexanderplatz*. This has not prevented seminars and doctoral theses from being written about my novel and its style at three universities. These are the typical judgments rife among the middle class and pedants about any writing that deviates from the "educated-cultivated" writing style found in living rooms of plush furniture. The justification states: "We must reject such corruption of the German language," well yes, he (or she) is absolutely correct, plenty of people would prefer to sit and sleep on plush furniture than to go out into the street and expose themselves to the fierceness of the unscented air. But that shouldn't prevent those of us who still serve art from writing as we wish and see fit, even in the face of such protestations from the repository of plush furniture and sideboards.

In fact, Serner's writing style is agile as a rapier, elegant, sharp, concise. It is an exemplary style in this genre, and the "justifier" is, again, completely clueless.

I hereby declare — and cannot deny that I am peeved by the provocative tone of the justification — my outrage that a good writer is being dragged before a tribunal as an author of "filth"! What the youth welfare offices should label as filth is their business. But to impugn the *literary reputation* of a good man in this way is an audacious step, and I would hope the Youth Welfare Office will not conceal its opinion from the "justifier."

Serner's novel is one among many. The justification, of course, reveals as little acquaintance with it as with other works in German literature. I have in front of me the five volumes of Serner's prose. I have known his work for a decade. He was one of the avant-gardists of Dadaism, etc. He is a genuine literary talent. His short stories, almost all of which are set in the same milieu as *The Tigress*, are truly exquisite gems. Serner's main strength lies in this form of small art, in his linguistic dexterity and precision in compact and incisive sketches. Painting epics in broad brush strokes is not exactly his forte.

As for the "filth," frankly, I fail to see it. A maidenly, chaste lexicon is not the norm in the underworld, and the style must be authentic, sharp, and clear. Handling this subject *without* utilizing what the justification calls filth — well, that is simply not possible. Whoever chooses this material (and whoever wishes to prohibit it), and whoever is an artist, cannot avoid all sorts of things that might displease all sorts of people. And if that be so, then the theme itself, the nature, is eradicated, or the art is banned. By way of criticism, it is pointed out that Fec "threw Bichette under him," and a "bed banging." To my mind the author did not tiptoe around the facts of the matter, and the manner of description is — as is always the case with Serner — concise and matter-of-fact, without a trace of lechery. How would the "justifier" have presented the facts in a more concise, more matter-of-fact way? (But he doesn't want the facts presented at all! I suppose we should roll back a few centuries for his sake, by court order.)

In contrast to the justification, I judge the novel *The Tigress* to be an excellent work of art — and in light of its naturalistic-amoral basic approach, a work devoid of any "filthy" (i.e., pornographic) intent.

[signed] Dr. Alfred Döblin
Author
Member of the Senate of the Prussian Academy of Arts
(Dept. of Poetry)

Notes

12 *"J'ai une femme qui aime les animaux, . . .":* "I have a wife who loves animals, that's funny, that's funny . . ."

48 *Paname:* slang for Paris, used here as well as a metonym for high society in general (likely in association with Parisians).

48 *Mistinguett:* stage name of Jeanne Florentine Bourgeois (1873-1956), theater and movie actress and singer, known especially for her engagements at Folies Bergère and Moulin Rouge. She was the most popular and highest-paid female entertainer of her era.

55 *La Valse brune:* the song was a fixture in Mistinguett's repertoire at Moulin Rouge.

146 *Other tabloids compared her . . . :* La Goulue was the stage name of Louise Weber (1866-1929) cancan dancer and star performer at Moulin Rouge; Grille d'Egout, contemporary of La Goulue and fellow cabaret cancan dancer; Jane Avril (1868-1943), born Jeanne Louise Beaudon, also a cancan dancer at Moulin Rouge and the subject of Henri de Toulouse-Lautrec's famous poster paintings, she was La Goulue's replacement, and unlike the other dancers kept her clothes on.

150 *the Berlin-N-Junge:* likely a reference to the black and biracial Afro-German youth who lived in Berlin, or it could be referring to one of the city's districts known for its youth movements and social clubs and general bohemian atmosphere.

161 *"anti-trash and -smut law":* the Gesetz zur Bewahrung der Jugend vor Schund- und Schmutzschriften [Law to Protect Youth from Trash and Smut Writings] was enacted by the German Reichstag on December 3, 1926, and went into effect two weeks later.

163 *he is a physician:* Döblin either believed Serner was indeed a doctor of medicine rather than of law, or he might have been ironically referring to when Serner forged a medical report in 1915 for his friend, the anarchist Franz Jung, to help him avoid having to serve at the front during WWI. This "favor" landed Serner in hot water with the police and, now a wanted man, was one of the reasons he subsequently fled to Zurich.

About the Translation

In the "Handbook of Practices" section of *Last Loosening*, Walter Serner created a practical playbook comprising 591 maxims for how to be a successful con artist, and many of these find their application in *The Tigress*. Serner depicts here, as he does with his crime stories, a demimonde that is authentic, edgy, and linguistically trenchant. Each of the two main protagonists (not to mention Pimpi) have their own particular ways of speaking, and the clash between them often gives rise to misunderstandings and general incomprehension. Whereas Fec's speech is, for the most part, somewhat more measured and logical, if not pedantic, even tending to ramble at times, Bichette's speech is more feral and idiosyncratic, clipped, her diction peppered with words not commonly in use or "off" in some way. With its mix of French and German dialect (and obscure at that, sometimes regional, sometimes Austrian), the German reader of the day would have likely found this quirky underworld patois disorienting, which was Serner's intent, but not entirely inaccessible. Such would not be the case for contemporary Anglophone readers. So we took the decision to find insofar as possible English equivalents for such oddities as "guips" (nettly), "schlingue" (rotter), "schlaß" (slack), "jus" (yak), and many others that would obviate the need to encumber the text with excessive notes while hopefully retaining an aspect of the strangeness, even if at the inevitable expense of somewhat mitigating the lexical anarchy.

To say the least, the translation was a joint effort. First and foremost, teasing out many meanings would have been nearly impossible without the seminal work of Thomas Milch on Serner's oeuvre, and the glossary he compiled is an invaluable resource. The translation had to be reworked in its entirety, and, where necessary, whole sections and chapters retranslated. The translator extends his thanks to the publisher's editorial team for their painstaking corrections and revisions, to Thomas Antonic and Malcolm Green for their suggestions and advice, and especially to Marisa Lourenço for her encouragement and support.

Bibliographic Note

The Tigress was originally published in German as *Die Tigerin. Eine absonderliche Liebesgeschichte* in two editions during Walter Serner's lifetime. The first was published by Elena Gottschalk Verlag, Berlin, in 1925; the second edition, perhaps with some minor alterations, was published by Paul Steegemann Verlag, Berlin, in 1927 as part of their seven-volume boxed set of Serner's collected work: *Die Bücher von Walter Serner*. More recent editions have drawn, as have this translation, on Thomas Milch's invaluable editorial work on Serner's entire oeuvre, published together as *Das gesamte Werk. Band 1-8, 3 Supplementbände*. (Munich: Renner, 1979-92). *Die Tigerin* appeared in 1980 as volume 3. The glossary compiled by Milch of Serner's more arcane slang and foreignisms informed many of the translation choices made herein. The additional texts included in our edition appeared in the Collected Works as volume 8 in 1984 under the title: *Der Abreiser. Materialien zu Leben und Werk*. They and other texts that more fully document the smear campaign unleashed against Serner and Lessing as well as additional "expert" testimonials are reproduced in the edition of *Die Tigerin* published by Arco Verlag (Wuppertal) in 2020, whose publisher was kind enough to provide us with a copy.

WALTER SERNER was born in 1889 as Walter Eduard Seligmann to a Jewish family in the western Bohemian town of Karlsbad (Karlovy Vary) where his father, Berthold Seligmann, owned the town's major newspaper, the *Karlsbader Zeitung*. Serner studied law in Vienna in 1913 and completed his doctorate at the University of Greifswald, before fleeing to Switzerland with the outbreak of World War I. He participated in Dada activities in Zürich, Geneva, and Paris, edited the magazines *Sirius* and *Zeltweg*, and composed his notorious Dada Manifesto, "Last Loosening," in 1918. By the early 1920s, he was traveling and living around Europe, alternately in Barcelona, Bern, Vienna, Karlovy Vary, and Prague, writing numerous crime stories and one novel, *The Tigress* (1925). In 1933, Serner's books were banned and burned by Nazi Germany. Having maintained a Czechoslovak passport since 1920, he ultimately settled in Prague and married his longtime partner, Dorothea Herz, in 1938. When Nazi Germany occupied Bohemia and Moravia in March 1939, the two unsuccessfully tried to escape to Shanghai. Serner and Herz were both transported in August 1942 to Terezín and from there "East" with other Jews from Bohemia, all of whom were summarily murdered and buried in a mass grave near Riga.

THE TIGRESS
A Curious Love Story
by Walter Serner

Translated from the original German
Die Tigerin. Eine absonderliche Liebesgeschichte
published in 1925 by Elena Gottschalk Verlag, Berlin

Initial translation by MK

Revised by TSP

Frontispiece by Leo Haas,
courtesy of the Jewish Museum in Prague

Cover image: "Marietta," 1916, oil on canvas
by Christian Schad, by permission of OOA-S

Layout and design by Silk Mountain

Text set in Garamond Premier Pro

FIRST EDITION

Published in 2025 by
Twisted Spoon Press
P.O. Box 21 — Preslova 12
150 00 Prague 5
Czech Republic
www.twistedspoon.com

Printed and bound in the Czech Republic by PROTISK

Distributed to the trade by

CENTRAL BOOKS
www.centralbooks.com

SCB DISTRIBUTORS
www.scbdistributors.com